I0602645

FADE
TO
BLACK

FADE
TO
BLACK

A MATT MOULTON MYSTERY

MICHAEL AMEDEO

First published by Level Best Books/Historia 2025

Copyright © 2025 by Michael Amedeo

All rights reserved. No part of this publication may be reproduced, stored or transmitted in any form or by any means, electronic, mechanical, photocopying, recording, scanning, or otherwise without written permission from the publisher. It is illegal to copy this book, post it to a website, or distribute it by any other means without permission.

This novel is entirely a work of fiction. The names, characters and incidents portrayed in it are the work of the author's imagination. Any resemblance to actual persons, living or dead, events or localities is entirely coincidental.

Michael Amedeo asserts the moral right to be identified as the author of this work.

First edition

ISBN: 978-1-68512-981-1

Cover art by Level Best Designs

This book was professionally typeset on Reedsy.
Find out more at reedsy.com

Chapter One

For a moment, I seemed to be lost in the dark.

I felt like a combination stuntman and movie director in the middle of a power outage. After all, the darkest part of night had set in, I stood in the middle of Hollywood balancing on the eighth story of a shaky, skeletal hotel fire escape, I held a modern camera in my mind, and I used it to follow the hot and heavy action in a room lit only by white walls and a silvery moon.

But my temporary confusion notwithstanding, I was neither stuntman nor director—I was a simple 35-year-old private dick named Matt Moulton carrying out a simple bedroom job, something to help pay the bills. My little camera took only still pictures. And had it been a real movie camera, the action I was capturing could never have made it to the big screen, even in the supposedly over-permissive modern age of today, October 1950. It was too blue, even in black and white.

But the pictures were certain to thrill my client, an avaricious little lady who was seeking a huge divorce settlement from her businessman husband. Each time I clicked the camera, I heard a cash register ching loudly in the ether (even all the car horns down below couldn't drown it out). Her now insignificant other, a triple-chinned graybeard of 45 or so with too much body hair and a plunging barrel for a belly, inserted his undersized member into a pale-skinned, squeaky-voiced blonde who looked less than half his age—and that was with the thick mask of cosmetics plastered on her sweetly round face. Without it, she might have been a high-school bobbysoxer sans the sox—and all other apparel, of course. Mr. Business approached the whole matter with the passion of a guy inking another contract. It was his secret bottom line. Well, it wasn't going to be secret any longer. At least one judge would be an interested viewer.

What made his mounting—or his business deal—so potentially rich and strange was that the guy's member was not alone in the blonde's most intimate of spaces. There was another, more hyperactive presence there. Better endowed and looking like a beige blackjack, it belonged to the gangly, younger gentleman that lay underneath her. Together, the fit seemed tight, and I couldn't help remembering the wise phrase "three's a crowd." Oh, definitely—the love nest was packed so snug it was almost squeaking.

It was what my Free French comrades in Vichy during the war would have called *ménage a trois*. They always bragged about having participated in one or witnessed one. Not I. Arguably oversexed Matt Moulton was completely virginal when it came to threesomes. I had never even seen one before.

Since sex times three might mean double the money, I was happy to keep shooting, though my feelings about the whole scene were mixed. I felt aroused and yet embarrassed. Naked bodies doing naughty things certainly appealed to my lustful instincts. But there was a right way and a wrong way to do things, including that natural thing people call lovemaking. Unfortunately, my three stars settled on a way that was too loud and discordant for me. In her hesitantly moaning falsetto, the blonde was singing a love song in which she didn't seem to know the words. My client's hubby was grunting and groaning in a repetitive rhythm that probably came out of the Neanderthal Swing era. And the skinny young guy proved so passionate about the goings-on above him that he was giving voice to all manner of sounds, from the shrilly exotic to the insanely alien. The threesome was doing anything but making beautiful music together, and they were doing it at such a volume that somebody was going to call the police. And snoopy, trouble-seeking gumshoes don't get along well with the cops, especially those of the officious LA variety. So, I finally packed up my camera of scandalous pictures and beat a very careful retreat down the flimsy metal stairway. I escaped. That is, the escape stayed intact long enough to guide me to the ground and out of that place. It was a cheaper hotel in a slightly run-down block, and I was sick of being there.

After the long day, I melted into the warm night, looking forward to spending the rest of my waking hours at home with a couple of drinks and a good book. But Fate didn't care what I wanted—it had its own plans for me. Before I could cross the street to reach my bluely beloved, relatively new Ford Club Coupe, I got squeezed. Two Negro linemen, dressed in pricey dark suits and homburgs, slammed into me, one on each side. They put their arms around my waist and started mouthing a conversational scat, seeking—no doubt—to convince passers-by that we were just good friends on a bender. Before I could do anything about the tackle, the massive guy on my right slipped his right hand under my jacket, removed my .38 Special, and dropped it into his pocket. I didn't see any of that; I just sensed it. He did it with the invisible precision of the best downtown pickpocket.

With the casual forcefulness, the kind of suppressed violence, of angry parents in public, they dragged me over to the family car, a maroon Cadillac. It looked a few weeks past brand new, but the embedded dirt on its whitewalls told me that these guys had come a long way. You don't pick up that much crud just driving back and forth a few times to Pasadena. The shorter, wider man on my left unlocked and opened the rear door and walked around to the driver's side. That invited man number two to practically pick me up and throw me into the rear seats. My head went hard into the left-side window. The window sustained the blow; it was my head that seemed to crack. With my mind in a spin, I paid little heed to my captor sitting down next to me.

I tried hard to focus on the specifics of the now, but all I could think about was how I was always boasting about being afraid of nothing. Of course, what that boast really meant was that I was afraid of everything because anything could lead to that nothing known as death. I was afraid to die. But my fear never paralyzed me—it just made me smarter, tougher, and more determined. I would do anything and everything to keep breathing. Now, whether it made sense or was meaningful to keep breathing, I couldn't say. I wasn't a philosopher. I was a dick that loved life, as hard, fragile, unfair, unjust, and random as it surely was. So as my mind finally spun to a stop, I took a shot at informing and defending myself with the best tool and most powerful weapon I had left: my big mouth.

"Okay, buddy boy, so we're long-lost brothers. It's nice to see you, how you been, and Mom sends her love. But now what gives with the rough stuff and the silent treatment? I don't take kindly to unprovoked nastiness," I said, with barely enough breath to get the last words out in the proper hardboiled tone. My head was still killing me.

His full-lipped mouth didn't crack a smile, but his big, round eyes hinted at one. He apparently found me amusing. It gave some much-needed expression to that giant sculpted face atop that impossibly huge body. If anyone ever said he was as big as a house, they definitely had the wrong real estate. He was a warehouse, an industrial one that was still growing (I was just happy I encountered him this year instead of next). And he actually deigned to speak with real information. Swallowing softly and partially closing his eyes, he said, in a surprisingly slight voice, "We're headed to your office now. We'll tell you more about our business there." His revelation greatly relieved me and then angered me a little as well. "Hey, pal, I have daytime office hours. I'm not a 24-hour drive in where you can just pick me up and pull me out anytime." His eyes danced with humor again. I guessed that the best thing to do was quit while I was ahead.

My black friends refused to give me much space. Even after we left the car, they insisted on holding my hands—or at least the arms connected to them—as we marched into the light gray stone office building on Sunset Boulevard near Western. It was a kind of senior citizen—in a city that was sprawling with newer and newer development and more and more people, this building just celebrated its twenty-fifth birthday. It seemed old by comparison with a lot of everything else. When the building came to be, Los Angeles was smaller, quieter, cleaner, less aggressive. It was called paradise back then, too, but the moniker was closer to reality in that day. Nineteen-fifty LA seemed like too much of a good thing, and I called that a bad thing. The excesses of the Hollywood industrial complex made it even worse. I preferred the Bay Area, where I started my career as a gumshoe, but as atmospheric and romantic as it was, the Bay Area certainly wasn't paradise either. I had to flee from there to save my life. You can't have a paradise when you have people. People bring greed, violence, jealousy, suspicion, revenge, resentment, narrow-mindedness, unbridled ambition, and power hunger to the scene. And I'm relieved they do. Without the dark side of humanity, which puts almost everything in shadow, I wouldn't have a job. So I fully embraced LA while always keeping a close eye out for its latest threat or outrage.

I toiled—did my best smoking and drinking—in a Spartan, eighth-floor, two-room office furnished with some of the best third-hand furniture that money could buy. My captors didn't seem very captivated by it—they spent their time rummaging through my metal desk drawers, apparently checking for stray guns or knives. All they could find was my letter opener, which I routinely used to pry the dirt from underneath my fingernails. They eyed it suspiciously but allowed me to put it back in my right drawer. Thank goodness!

I opened the blinds and the window to let some of the buzzing streetlight in—it gave the place atmosphere. I also pushed a second client chair beside my desk. "Will you gentlemen please have a seat? You're getting me nervous with your endless pacing around. And while you're sitting down, I'm going to go mix myself a badly needed drink. Would you like one, too?"

"No, we don't drink while we're working," said the warehouse man, with little conviction.

"Aw, c'mon, relax and have a drink. I've completely run out of poison, and so you won't have to worry about that."

The big man seemed amused again. "Okay, give us a couple of short ones."

I poured them a couple of long ones, and no one objected. I gulped down mine, poured myself another, and then sat down with my cigarette case in hand. "Would you guys like a smoke?" They shook their heads no in unison. I fired up mine and took a long and contented drag. They sipped their drinks and finally seemed satisfied. That was good bourbon.

"Now tell me your names and why you dragged me into doing more overtime. What's your story? What's the pitch?" I peered at them through the fog of smoke.

Warehouse removed his hat, took another sip, and then spoke in his high-volume whisper. "I'm Josh, and my partner's Lincoln. We've come to see you on behalf of Rose Fischetti. She needs you to do a very important personal job," he said, as if that told the whole story. Lincoln also took off his homburg, exposing an impeccably polished head without hair.

Fischetti? The name was familiar, but I couldn't place it at first. It sounded like Italian organized crime. But how could that be? Was the mob getting liberal in its middle age, hiring black men as its soldiers? Tolerance and the mafia—I couldn't believe it. "Who the Hell is Rose Fischetti, and where does she come from?"

"She operates out of Chicago," said Josh, again sounding as if that's all I needed to know.

"Chicago? The place that's only 2,000 miles away? Why doesn't she hire a detective in Chicago? That city is full of dicks. Why come to me?" I said, in a slightly outraged wonder about Rose's Chicago, the place where I was born and raised.

"She needs you." He took another sip.

Suspicion was my better half, and it was nagging me right

now. "Is Rose Fischetti part of organized crime? I don't do illegal things for clients, especially involving violence."

"No, Rose Fischetti is not part of the police," clarified Josh.

I snickered. "Oh, I like you, Josh, you're funny. The police as organized crime? Unfortunately, that's sometimes true—I've seen it firsthand. You took a nice shot there. Now, would you guys like another shot of whisky?"

Josh raised his eyes in surprise. "Oh yeah, okay, a couple of short ones." It was that short fiction again. Lincoln swigged the rest of his glass to make room for more. I poured them a couple of long ones. We were all comfortable.

I puffed out a smoke ring. "But you still haven't told me much. What does Rose want me to do? And again, it's got to be totally above board. Or at least very close to it...."

"Everything will be totally legit," said Josh. "But Rose will have to meet with you and explain the job. I'm not authorized to do that."

He removed a white envelope from his breast pocket, pulled out its cash content, and counted out ten new one-hundred-dollar bills on my desk. He did it with the unconscious style of someone who's worked with a lot of money before. "This would be your first payment. Mrs. Fischetti would also pay for all your expenses. When the job's done, she would pay you at least another thousand dollars as final compensation." He also smiled.

I felt like the alcoholic who knows he better not take the drink, but who wants the glass anyway. I felt as uncomfortable about this job as I did about that last big one in the Bay Area a year ago. But why? Was it because I knew nothing about what Fischetti wanted? Or was it because I was seized by a sixth sense that Fate was too dangerous to mess with this time? I decided in favor of the middle ground—I would take a little sip rather than drink the whole glass. I'd talk to Fischetti first, and then I'd make the final decision whether to accept the job. In the meantime, I slipped that cool thousand into my wallet. "Okay, where do I meet Mrs. Fischetti?" I didn't know what to do with the rest of the cigarette, and so I slowly, thoughtfully twisted it out in the tray.

"You need to go to Chicago as soon as possible. When can you leave?" said Josh, in his loudest and most earnest whisper.

"Do you mind if I take a train? I'd leave on the Super Chief tomorrow night and probably arrive in Chicago by early afternoon on Friday. Where do I go?"

He took the pen and pad off my desk and wrote something down. "This is Mrs. Fischetti's head...ah, home address." He handed me the pad.

"Oh, she lives on the South Side of the city, not far from where I went to college."

For the first time, Josh seemed intensely interested in what I was saying. "Where did you go to college?'

"The University of Chicago, in the Hyde Park neighborhood."

"Oh no, that place is far, far away," he assured me.

I didn't know why he said that. The university was just a few miles away. But I wasn't going to debate a current Chicagoan on the city's geography. I had more urgent things in mind. "Okay, where's my gun? I don't work without it."

He pulled my gun out of his pocket, pointed it menacingly at me, rolled his eyes, and reluctantly placed it on my desk. I guessed he was showing me his passive-aggressive side.

"Now, would you gentlemen drive me to my car?"

"We can't. We're in a hurry to drive back to Chicago. You can take a taxi and charge it to Mrs. Fischetti."

I stood up, grabbed my gun, and pointed it at them this time. They started to stir without moving, but before anyone got too upset, I slipped it into my holster. I then shook each man's hand and said: "Josh, Lincoln, it was just too marvelous for words. Thanks for nothing." My new playmates left.

The office clock said 2:00 in the morning, and that meant it was either too late or too early to call Sara Manson, my assistant. I didn't want to wake her two children or her big-kid, perpetually unemployed husband, but I dialed her up anyway. I had to prepare her for tomorrow's arrangements. After a half dozen rings, someone answered.

"Ahh, hello, what is it? said the woozy female voice.

"Hi Sara, it's Matt! How are you? I'm very sorry to disturb you, but I've got a big job that I need you to get started on first thing in the morning."

"Is anything wrong, Matt?" Sara was good at reading me, even over the phone.

"I don't think so. But I'll need to leave for Chicago tomorrow and probably spend a couple days there. You'll need to reserve a bedroom for me on the Super Chief."

"Oh, will you visit your parents?"

"Yeah, I'll see Mom and Dad for an evening. But the real reason for the trip is to look up a high-priced client named Rose Fischetti. I need you to find out more about her through public sources and through my Chicago detective friend, Tom Hartley. I suspect that she's somehow tied in with organized crime, but I don't know that for a fact."

"It sounds like it could be dangerous."

"Well, the job pays a small fortune, and that usually means it's potentially high-risk. But maybe not. Please see what you can find out, sweetheart. Good night or good morning, whichever one you prefer."

Right now, I felt stuck in the Great In-Between.

Chapter Two

Everybody always talked about the "perfect" weather in LA—the abundant sunshine and the bone-dry warmth. I partly agreed with that idea—the weather was perfect for driving to the coastal areas and beachcombing. Young women wore their shortest shorts there, and that itself made for a kind of limited paradise. But what do you do when you have to make a living in that weather, when you have to wrap yourself in a suit jacket and knot a tie around your neck? Well, you sweat, and you sweat, and you sweat. You feel like a steam room attendant in woolens. Among my clients, even those from the sometimes-air-conditioned confines of Beverly Hills and Brentwood, the most common sign of everyday, Southern California life was the drip-soaked armpit in the dress or jacket, the drenched fabric pasted to the lower back. And what did it feel like for women to wear girdles and nylon stockings in that weather? You could get wet just thinking about it. As I prepared to begin a new day, heading for the office in the heat, I looked forward to a couple of days in the more business-friendly clime of the chilled Windy City.

But I hated to leave home—my little fifth-floor apartment in a modern, rose-colored building on Wilshire Boulevard. The place unfolded in a jazzy, improv-like curve, and it offered things I never had in an apartment before: a couple of floor-to-ceiling windows, a wide balcony, a turquoise dining room (that I used as a gaudy second office), and plumbing that actually worked every day. The pretentious would call it "chic" or "chi-chi." But I saw it as my "clean, well-lighted place," my sanctuary from a world of dirty toil and dangerous trouble. The only drawback was the rent—I had to come up with a C-note every month. That meant I had to work longer and harder and pitch for pricier jobs that—like the Fischetti case—posed perhaps a greater challenge but also much more risk. The trick was to maintain a working balance and not let the high cost of living be dying. Fate wouldn't necessarily help me there.

With an overcoat and a little suitcase in the back seat, I drove to the office in my sun-drenched Ford, noontime traffic turning a 10-minute walk into a half-hour motor crawl. But I didn't grouse about it, because I was eager to see what Sara had put together about Rose Fischetti. I always expected the world from Sara, and she always delivered not only that but also the atmosphere surrounding it. For in addition to being an efficient secretary and assistant, she was a crack researcher that dug for information like the most dogged journalist. But if she had the mind of a reporter, she had the instincts of a gumshoe. I could bounce ambiguous clues and vague facts off her, and they'd come back as credible insights. She essentially served as my investigator behind the desk—my female dick—and she loved it. An excited, faraway look flashed in her big brown eyes when I told her of my dangerous experiences and misadventures—she seemed to relive them. And knowing I was a deadeye with a gun, she regularly arranged for me to take her shooting—maybe someday it would be her shot that made a difference, or so I believed she imagined. The best move I ever made was when I took Sara and her family along with me when I relocated to Los Angeles. I would never have been able to find a replacement for her here or anywhere.

Sara was a statuesque, bottle-blonde, flirting with forty. She wore figure-enhancing clothes with conservative designs and colors. She smiled a lot and spoke softly and sweetly, but none of that could completely hide the edge and the attitude of the inner lady. Probably without realizing it, Sara was auditioning for the part of private eye, albeit a slightly softer, reconfigured version. In a different time or a different world, she would have won the part.

I strolled into the office at the right time—it smelled as if Sara had just made a pot of her potent coffee. It was better because it was bitter, with a touch of sweetness from the cinnamon she sprinkled into the mix. "Hello sweetheart, how's business?"

"Hi, Matt. I've been in the library or on the phone all day. But nothing came in between those times." She occupied space in the office, but her mind seemed to be someplace else, miles away—two thousand miles away, to be exact. "Would you like some coffee, Matt?"

"Yes, I couldn't live without it." She pantomimed a laugh, poured me a cup, and placed it on her desk next to the client chair. She knew what the first order of business had to be. I sat down in the chair and fired up a cigarette. I knew she wouldn't want one right now.

"Your train for Chicago departs at 7:00 tonight. You'll return to LA on the 3:00 train on Sunday afternoon. Will that be enough time for you?"

"For now, that seems right. But we'll see what Fischetti has in mind for me."

"Yes, that brings me to my research. A Rose by any other

name would be an ordinary, wealthy client. But you were right about this one—she's planted in the greener pastures of organized crime. Rose is a gang leader by marriage—twenty-five years ago, she wed the Italian Mob leader Louis Fischetti."

"That's right—Louis Fischetti! I remember that name from childhood, from the time my dad covered the crime beat for the Tribune."

"Rose was a sultry, 17-year-old chanteuse in one of his South Side jazz clubs in 1925, and the 31-year-old Louis reportedly fell hard for her at first sight. Ding, dong, ding—wedding bells rang a few days later," said Sara, with a mocking tone. "But actually, according to your detective friend Hartley, the marriage made the wild-child Louis more serious about business. Initially confined to bootlegging and gambling, he also took on prostitution and drugs and spread his influence into many more neighborhoods—always, of course, with the permission of kingpin Al Capone. When his dad Vito died in 1931, Louis inherited the rest of the Fischetti empire—which included legitimate businesses—and probably tripled his wealth."

"Big, big man...for a while," I felt compelled to add.

"Exactly, Matt. A heart attack reduced him to dust just nine years later, at the age of 46."

"Forget about socialism, sweetheart—death is the best, most efficient equalizer."

Sara's laugh came with a pinch of discomfort. I didn't like the truth either.

"Rose took over everything and apparently found it wanting. She expanded on her husband's expansions, reaching into growing Negro neighborhoods, such as the prized, middle-class Bronzeville section of the South Side. She had a clearer and freer field there and other places because the Feds had taken Capone out of the picture. Other gangs opposed her aggressiveness, but Rose was ruthless. Some of her key foes in politics and crime suddenly disappeared or lost their lives in freak accidents. Meanwhile, she eluded the police and foiled the DA—she's never been charged with so much as a misdemeanor." Sara sat back and relaxed. "Could I have a cigarette now?"

I offered her one from my case and lit it for her. "So that's my potential new client? I don't know if I want her kind of trouble. Did you gain any insight into what she might want me to do for her?"

She blew smoke toward our sooty ceiling. "No, nothing stood out as potential dick work. But you've only heard maybe half the story."

"You mean, you have a lot more?"

"Well, it's significant, but it's short and sweet: Rose is black."

I choked on my coffee and started coughing violently. Sara stood up and pounded on my back. "Are you okay, Matt, are you okay?"

"Yes," I said through the dissolving clot of liquid in my throat. I forced a couple of coughs to complete the job. "The shock shook up my plumbing, sending the java down the wrong pipe." I spent a few long seconds trying to recover from the irony of it all. "It's something that even Hollywood wouldn't dare dream up: A black woman controlling an Italian mob. "

"Well, let's not exaggerate it, Matt. Remember that Rose expanded into Black areas and took on a lot of Negro manpower. The composition of the Fischetti gang today might be about fifty percent Italian, fifty percent Black."

"That makes it even more amazing. In Chicago, at least, the

Italian mob is now integrated."

Sara laughed. She liked my idea but thought it needed a shave. "It took them a while to get there, and only after a lot of kicking and screaming. The gangster community initially took offense at Louis's marriage to Rose. For years, rival gangs seemed to revel at hitting the Fischetti mob especially hard over every little bit of contested influence and real estate. At one point, someone left a burning cross on Louis and Rose's front lawn. No ordinary neighbor would have dared do that. The newspapers said that it was the work of either a rival gang or— the preferred idea—a disgruntled group within the Fischetti mob."

"Was there any suspicion that gangland Rose haters killed Louis?"

"The police and the press insisted the cause of death was all heart."

I needed a real drink. I got up, poured a short one, and swallowed it down. "I don't understand. Why does anyone care about the skin color of someone's mate?"

Sara knew I knew the answer—and the personal way I was looking at it. So she tried to reassure me with the truth. "Well, Matt, you know how intolerant people can be about race. You unfortunately experienced that firsthand."

I wanted to change the subject without looking like I was doing it. "If Rose could force Italian mobsters to play nice with blacks and share the benefits of stealing, gambling, pimping, streetwalking, and drug dealing, she's one tough broad. But if she wants me to flesh out her internal opponents, I'm not her kind of guy. I can't afford to antagonize any more mobs."

Eyes lowered and forehead crinkled, Sara wore her look of worry. 'It might not start out as that kind of job. But, as you know from the Bay Area experience, these jobs can take on a life of their own and develop a dangerous momentum into unexpected places."

"Well, sweetheart, where there's life, there's hope," I said in my best tone of mocking irony. But I got Sara's point: I'd better watch where I was going.

Chapter Three

I felt soft and a little guilty. For two-and-a-half days on the high-speed Super Chief train, I had enjoyed a life of uninterrupted luxury and ease, sleeping in a private bedroom, spending a lot of time in an ornate lounge car with expensively clever drinks, and eating fresh and delicious meals that my richer clients would have called fine dining. It was like staying in a high-class hotel that never stopped moving. After all that indulgence, was I now ready to take on any tough challenges? My first test came when I emerged from Chicago's Union Station. Sagging dark clouds crowded the sky, the temperature felt like it was a few degrees north of freezing, an aggressive drizzle pelted the streets, and an icy wind gushed in from Lake Michigan. It was a little more weather than I had bargained for. But no problem: I wandered around in that atmosphere for only a long half hour—the time it took to finally find and flag down an empty taxi on the congested streets. I had thought that everybody in Chicago took the elevated.

Wet and chilled like a bottle of cheap wine on ice, I sat in the cab watching the passing places and people and musing about my abandoned hometown. While Chicago wasn't as new and dynamic as LA, its size, energy, and striking lakefront geography made it one of the great cities. Both places pushed development, with LA growing out into a sprawl toward the ocean and Chicago growing up toward the stars (the real ones). Chicago was a vertical city: Towering buildings dotted the downtown and spread North and South along the lakefront. That didn't make it better than lower-rise LA—it just gave it a notably different personality. If Chicago held one distinctive advantage, though, it was in being more weathered than LA (and I'm not just talking about the wind and cold). It had a lot more hard-nosed, down-in-the-dirt experience in successfully conducting business and organizing crime. I worried solely about the latter, but developments would prove that to be shortsighted. The job would take on a life of its own—and where had I heard that idea?

The cab ride had gone on for too long when we finally reached 47th Street, the main drag of the black Bronzeville neighborhood and the most recent focus of the Fischetti mob's expansion. The old street—which needed repaving here and there—bustled with establishments desperate to separate people from their money, with grocery stores, clothing shops, movie theaters, beauty salons, bars, restaurants, and nightclubs leading the way. And that was the neighborhood's visible economy; the other economy, hiding and operating behind it, was the one the Fischettis exploited and controlled. Part of the invisible suddenly made an afternoon appearance when a voluptuous streetwalker in gaudy clothes jaywalked in front of my cab and almost got herself killed. The cabbie screamed at her with the suppressed fury of someone who had been driving too many hours for too many days. But I couldn't get too mad at her; she was just a careless young woman who—like all of us—was trying to make a living the best way she knew how. Besides, she was cute.

Off 47th, we turned down the residential street of Rose's address. The homes were relatively uniform, on both sides of the street, as far as the eye could see. They were older two- and three-story homes, modestly built and still well maintained, with no lawns or just patches of one and an occasional, now orangey-leaved tree. But then suddenly, as I looked out on my right, I thought my vision was blurring. I seemingly saw the same four or so light-brown brick houses blending together as one. But I wasn't drunk, and my eyes turned out to be okay; This really was one new home, and it was gang leader Rose's address. Rather than drop a mansion onto this middle-class street, Rose took modesty to luxurious lengths, building an ordinary-looking two-story building on multiple lots. It was her sprawling version of the postwar middle-class American Dream, nicer lawn and larger garage included.

I left the taxi and approached the Rose residence. I hadn't taken three steps before I drew a crowd of three trouble-seeking young men, part of the Fischetti guard, no less. Two were White, one was Black. The White spokesmen, mean-looking in a very effeminate way, blew his stale Sen-Sen breath into my face and said, "What's your business, darling? This is restricted ground around here."

"I'm the postman making a special delivery," I cracked.

The guy looked me over with the confused suspicion of a surly, know-it-all bully-boy who could never get the joke, never take the hint. He inspected my dark coat with a turned-up collar and my light-gray suit, black shirt, and light-gray tie. By the time his eyes reached up to my bent-brimmed black fedora, he realized I was no mailman. His mouth curled down, and his fist balled up, and he was ready to hit me. "Okay, okay, blue eyes, turn down the heat—you'll live longer," I said. "I come in

21

peace; your boss wants to see me."

"Rose Fischetti? he densely asked.

"That is the one."

"What's your name?

"Matt Moulton. You want me to spell it?"

"Wait here." As he headed toward the stairs, I shouted out: "Hurry, please. It's wet out here, and my clothes aren't drip-dry." He turned and shot me a bullet of a look. It hurt my feelings.

I turned around and sought solace from his friends, but they wouldn't even look at me. They were too busy trying to appear busy, scraping the sidewalk with their shoes.

Bully boy returned and assured me I was okay. Energized by this discovery of a lifetime, I went up the rubber-carpeted stairs and rang the bell. A smiling white man in a black suit quickly opened the double door. "Mr. Moulton? Please come in. Let me take your coat and hat." His build was forcefully broad, with a chest like Superman's. His accent was distinctly British, like something out of the movies. And his manner was helpfully gracious with a slight detour toward the ominous. I couldn't figure out if he was a butler or a bodyguard. And then I found out he was both.

"I apologize, Mr. Moulton, but I'm going to need to frisk you. We maintain strict security around here. May I?"

"Sure, go ahead. But I warn you that you'll find a gun under my jacket." During the frisk, he removed my .38. with seeming regret. "I'll keep your weapon with your hat and coat in the closet. Thank you for your understanding, Mr. Moulton. Now, please take a seat. Would you like a drink?"

I felt that this was one butler to whom you didn't say "no." Besides, I was thirsty. "Sure, I thought you'd never ask. I'll take a scotch and water."

"Right away, sir," said the Brit, and he was off to the races.

The Rose residence was a tale of two homes. On the outside, it worked hard to look everyday and pedestrian, in its blown-up kind of way. But on the inside, it relaxed and slipped into something more comfortable: twenty-four-carat gold. The large drawing room flowed into a parlor, both plushly carpeted and decorated with expensive and exotic European furniture. The appealingly unconventional, odd-shaped sofas, chairs, lamps, and tables matched the coloring on the walls. Each room had a two-color theme: The drawing room was red and black, and the parlor was a subdued green and yellow. I sat on a long and narrow red wool sofa with a pillowed black back. It afforded the kind of luxury and comfort that could cloud your mind. So I paid greater attention to the painting of a generic countryside that hung on the wall behind the sofa. The big room's only big weakness, it was less an artwork than a colorful decoration, a department-store product to quickly fill an empty wall. It was thoughtless: With all that money, the Fischettis should have been able to afford real art, like a portrait or two from Reginald Marsh.

Jeeves appeared out of nowhere with my drink on a silver platter. "Mr. Moulton, Mrs. Fischetti is ready to see you now. Please follow me." We walked up a wide spiral staircase to the second floor. That brought us to another living room, this one featuring the usual Euro furniture, a large television console, and a modern hi-fi with the great Billie Holiday's smoky voice curling out of it. Billie was crooning "Crazy He Calls Me," and I wondered if the song had personal significance to my client. While her mob opponents no doubt called her crazy, they couldn't stop her from racing past them to the top.

The butler led me into a smaller, darker room where Rose Fischetti sat behind a polished wood desk, her hands folded into a seeming prayer grip and her amber-colored eyes lost in a search for something that wasn't there. My presence roused her back to reality, or whatever we called this state we lived in every day. She stood up, mustered a half smile, and gripped my hand. "Oh, I'm sorry, Mr. Moulton. I'm pleased to meet you. Please take a seat." I was tired of sitting, but I followed orders.

She exuded real authority, a kind of silent power. That told me that it had been years in the making. According to Sara, the very young Rose was gorgeous, seductive, and charming, and that gave her sexual power over men, most especially Louis, who would become her mate. During the years of her marriage, she wielded a different kind of power, one where she could acquire whatever she wanted whenever she wanted it. After Louis died, and she took over the reins, Rose returned to exerting authority over men, but this time she drove them with a carefully planned combination of force and violence. She learned well, and her power evolved and expanded. I guessed that she had no second thoughts about it—dominance had just become second nature to her. I sipped her premium scotch and waited to hear where that power was taking her right now.

She sat back in her chair, folded her hands together under her chin, and narrowed her eyes in my direction. Her face was still nice to look at, graced by large, widely spaced eyes, an upturned nose, pouting lips, and silky brown skin. The problems were the ravages of time, the pressures of power, and perhaps the dissipations of high living. They left their mark with a web of eye wrinkles that couldn't be covered by makeup, slightly padded cheeks that made her face look fuller than she probably wanted, a hairline that was heading North, and an emerging second chin that, considering her relative youth, was a premature birth. Rose's beauty hadn't wilted, but the elements were working on it.

"Thank you for coming all the way out to Chicago, Mr. Moulton. I appreciate the fact that you've agreed to work with me," she said, her head slightly nodding for emphasis.

"I don't want to be difficult, Mrs. Fischetti, but let me make it clear that I haven't agreed to do anything yet. I'm here to just hear you out. I told your two messengers that I don't do violence or anything knowingly illegal. If that's the work you need done, I'd be happy to refund your thousand and return to LA." I killed my drink.

She crossed her arms against her chest and looked at me in cold silence for a few seconds. "If I wanted that kind of help, I wouldn't have sent for you. My people can take care of that kind of stuff quite well, thank you." She was getting a little impatient.

"Oh, I'm sure of that, Mrs. Fischetti."

She noticed my empty glass. "I apologize, would you like another drink?"

"Not now, thank you."

Rose paused to get her main thoughts back. "What I want from you is much more important. I need you to find my little girl," she said, her voice breaking.

"You lost your little girl? Why didn't you go to the police?"

She was dismissive. "They can't do anything for me. I need a professional." Her eyes began to water.

"I feel bad for you. But I don't run a lost kid service. I wouldn't even know how to go about it."

She removed a handkerchief from her desk and dabbed her eyes, taking some eye shadow along with it. "Julie is twenty-three years old, Mr. Moulton."

"Well, why didn't you tell me that? I can certainly help you with missing people who have been out of diapers for a while. When and where did she disappear? Tell me the whole story."

"Julie started out like I did, singing in a Fischetti jazz nightclub. She drew good, enthusiastic crowds to the Cocoa Club, a place a few blocks from here, just off 47th Street. But she pined away for much more—the opportunity to become a Hollywood star like Lena Horne. That was all she talked about, day and night. Finally, two-and-a-half years ago, she packed up and took off for Los Angeles, taking her penniless, no-account boyfriend with her."

"Who is he?"

"His name is Michael Sykes; he was the piano player in the Cocoa Club band. He's a pleasant and good-looking guy, but he's shiftless, somebody who's just not good enough for my daughter. But he suddenly found some ambition and convinced himself that he could get into the pictures, too. If he had stayed, she would have stayed, too. So I partly blame him for her departure...and disappearance." Her face stayed calm, but her body seemed to tense for war. And then tears started creeping out again.

"Mrs. Fischetti, they went out to LA, and then what happened? Did they give you an address, the place where they were living?"

"Oh yeah, they shacked up together in an apartment on Jefferson Boulevard. I called Julie there every day, and we talked. And within a few months, she actually started to realize her dream: Viogram Pictures signed her to a contract. One thing led to another, and the studio put her in a real picture, a race film called 'Living the Blues.' I felt so proud seeing her, bigger than life, singing and dancing on the movie screen in her one scene. She looked like a future star.

"Months later, the studio gave her another part, a much smaller one as a native girl in the jungle movie 'Man of the Wild.' After that, for more than a year, she didn't work at all. There was nothing. Viogram kept assuring her a new role was coming, but they never delivered on their promise. Of course, Julie became severely depressed. Every other time I called, she'd start crying, or she and Michael would break out into an argument. And then..." Rose tried to stifle a sob.

"Yes, Mrs. Fischetti...?

"And then, I could no longer reach her by phone—I found out that their line was disconnected. My letters to her came back as undeliverable. She apparently moved without leaving a forwarding address. My little girl just disappeared...."

"Had you and Julie argued or disagreed about something during your last call?"

"In those last months, we always disagreed: I advised her to come back home, and she insisted that she'd miss her big chance if she left now. We argued, but it never became bitter—I don't think that was part of our relationship."

"When was the last time you talked to her?"

"Two months ago—August 2nd."

"Was Michael working at all during their time in LA?

"I don't know if he had signed a contract with Viogram, but he did land a small role in "Living the Blues" as a piano player in a couple of scenes."

"What money were they living on?"

"Well, her contract paid for the two roles and advanced her additional funds after that. But in the unemployed last year before the disappearance, I had to send her checks on a regular basis. They lived off that money." She stared into the ether again.

"Mrs. Fischetti, I've been dicking in Los Angeles for only a year, but I've seen and heard countless cases of Midwestern kids chasing fame and fortune in Hollywood and losing themselves in the pursuit. To achieve success there, all a kid needs is everything—good looks, a vague ability to perform, obsessive determination, inside contacts, and—most important—a lot of dumb luck. And you know what? Most of the time, having all of that is still not enough. Once a guy or girl learns the truth, it's sometimes too late or too depressing or too shameful to go back home and start over."

"But my Julie is both beautiful and talented. Let me show you some of her pictures." Rose spread glamor pictures on the desk before me.

They showed that Julie had a real talent...for posing. She seemed self-consciously pretty, with a shapely, heavily made-up face featuring big brown eyes, carefully winged eyebrows, and full lips. Her hair was straight and cut fashionably close to the head, and her skin was unusually light, though it wouldn't "pass"—as they say—for white. She was the color of premium coffee with a lot of cream.

"Your daughter has the looks, but what about the contacts and what about the luck? And I forgot to mention one other thing she needs—the right skin color. If the odds are 500-1 against the average pretty and talented white girl making it as even a minor star, the odds triple or quadruple against the pretty and talented black girl. It's not impossible to make it, as you showed with your mention of Lena Horne. I could name a few others. But black success is close to improbable in modern-day Hollywood, and I don't think I have to tell you that."

"No, no, Mr. Moulton, you don't. I used to say that to Julie again and again...."

"While I don't want to alarm and distress you, there's something else you have to consider. You've made a lot of enemies. Some tough people don't like your business practices and—perhaps most important—don't like the temerity of a Negro woman beating them at their own game. Could one of your opponents have harmed or kidnapped Julie to get back at you?"

Guilt crossed her face—but it didn't stop. "No, I don't think so. This war has been going on for a long while. If my enemies were going to hurt Julie, wouldn't they have tried it when she was younger and more vulnerable? Why would they have waited until now?"

"I can't answer that. But one thought comes to mind: It would be harder for you to trace a hostile action that takes place 2,000 miles away. Bad people can hurt Julie while remaining anonymous."

"I would never totally rule out that possibility, Mr. Moulton. But," she said in a raised and roused voice, "if my enemies did do harm to Julie, fuck them: I will hammer them, dismember them, and feed their remains to the wild dogs." The scary thing was that she wasn't exaggerating.

"For right now, though, I have to focus on the more realistic likelihood that she disappeared voluntarily. Or if not voluntarily, that she is at least still alive somewhere and can be saved. I need you, Mr. Moulton. You've worked on the problem of foolish people losing themselves in the chase for Hollywood fame. And you would bring a special sympathy to this case."

"Special sympathy, Mrs. Fischetti? What do you mean?

"Sympathy and understanding are qualities that make you stand out. You dated a Negro woman for years—if push came to shove, you wouldn't suddenly abandon Julie's case because of her skin color."

Chapter Four

As Rose kept talking about my special sympathy, I fell into a reverie about her "Negro woman" comment. She was right: I dated a black woman named Gina Harner for more than two years in the Bay Area. We created our own, fanciful little world, but we went too far with it: We fell in love. In fact, Gina was probably the only woman I ever truly loved.

But this story began just after the war, when I used my so-called heroics as a sniper in occupied France to land a job as a detective with the San Francisco police. The job taught me a lot about crime and corruption, mainly the kind of stuff that often went on within the detective bureau itself. The lieutenant—a crew-cut, oily-faced belligerent by the name of Brannigan—ran the department like his own personal dictatorship. He kowtowed only to more powerful and more corrupt others, such as the mayor, the police chief, and the DA. As one of his detectives, you didn't always have to obey the law, but you did have to follow orders—no matter how unreasonable—and adhere to all the nitpicking rules of the department, filling out this and filling out that, in triplicate, of course. It was wicked, intense, and dreary. I liked the job as much as a bad toothache—on each side of the mouth.

But the detective bureau was where I met Gina, whose presence eased some of the pain. She worked as the administrative secretary: Everything that went into and out of the department passed through her. While she didn't manage anyone or investigate anything, she kept track of where the detectives were sent and where the case files were stored—in other words, she knew where all the bodies were buried. She did her job smartly, but the problem was that she did it beautifully as well. It was her earthly beauty that drew all the staring and the flirting and the whispering from other detectives, all of whom were white. "Well, she's a Negro so she must be loose, right?" went the direction of the commentary. With all that focus on her, I tried to stay away at first. But that effort proved futile. How could I resist someone who was like the morning time in human form? Gina had a fresh face, bright light brown eyes, and saucy lips, and she radiated a kind of raw and warming energy. It so animated her long legs and curvy hips that she seemed to be dancing as she walked. It was all so natural.

One day I spotted nature woman sitting alone in the cafeteria, and I asked her if she wanted some company.

"Sure, Matt—as long as you promise not to be too interesting. I don't want to be distracted from my life's work." She winked and smiled.

"Nah, don't worry, Gina, I'm not corrupt enough to be interesting."

"I don't need the corruption—I just like to watch you smoke."

"Watch me smoke?"

"Matt, no one does it with more style than you do. It looks like you're playing jazz. You give it a rhythm, but then you improvise here and there with an unusual drag and puff."

I laughed, took out a cigarette, and lit it. But now I felt self-conscious. "Well, you play a mean keyboard on the typewriter."

"Yeah, 'Stormy Weather' at 55 words per minute."

"That's too fast. Say, as long as we're getting personal, how can you stand those creepy cops coming on to you all the time? I know you're attractive, but that doesn't give them the right to spout off about it with sexual and racial insinuations. I know I get offended."

"Really? I don't. They're just white boys fantasizing about something they know they can't have because they can no longer just take it. I just smile at their remarks and then roll my eyes—in my head."

"Yeah, but their crap ruins it for other guys who may have a serious and honorable interest in you. How can those other guys even dare approach you after you've put up with all of that?"

She gave me an "I see through you" beam. "Who are these other guys?"

"Well, it's actually just one guy, a detective."

"A detective? Does he have a heart?"

"No, he doesn't have a heart, but he's a real nice guy and he thinks you're the tops."

"Well, maybe I can find him a good used one. Tell him to call me." I fell in love with her at that moment.

We saw a lot of each other after that, uniquely becoming both buddies and beloveds. One minute we'd be cracking wise about things usually not shared in polite boy-girl company. The next minute, we'd be taking romance for a spin with a souped-up passion. Yes, your Honor, we were guilty of speeding. And yes, driving without a license, too.

But the issue of race always followed us around. As we went

about the city together, we turned a lot of heads, with a few too many of the faces showing disapproval and even contempt.

One day, we visited one of the Bay Area's most popular live swing-music clubs, seemingly a very liberal and open-minded place. It was a Saturday night, and so we had to wait in line to get a table or booth. After a long while, Gina took off for the ladies' room. Then I heard the guy from the couple in front of us say he forgot his pack of cigarettes in the car. Once he left, his mate—a faded highfalutin blonde with too much eye shadow—turned around and tried to chat. It had the air of a flirt session.

"How about this wait? The place better be good."

"Oh, it is. The music is smokin', and the drinks are dynamite."

She looked me over as if she were undressing me and then took a thoughtful drag on her cigarette. "Wow, with all the boys having come back home, it must be tough."

"I don't know what you mean."

"You know, the woman shortage. There aren't enough good women to go around. You have to settle for what's left over if you want to have a little fun."

"I still don't know what you mean." But I knew exactly what she was struggling to say.

"You know, a good-looking guy like you is reduced to going dark. Now, if you ask me...."

"Hey, dollie, I'm not asking you. I'm not buying what you're selling. Peddle your puss somewhere else."

"I beg your pardon, what are you trying to say?"

"I'm telling you to turn around."

"We'll see what my husband has to say about this."

"If he's anything like you, I'll send him home with a black eye, a broken nose, and a tail between his legs." The ugly incident ended there.

In our travels, we sometimes even got disapproving, if much more subtle, reactions from black people. The American world was essentially shaking its head and wagging its finger at us, railing away that the romantic pairing of a White man and a Negro woman was freakish and maybe illicit. And this was happening in the middle of the 20th century, right after the victory in the vaunted war for democracy.

If the outside world's reaction was bad, the bureau's was worse, especially from a guy like Brannigan. That wasn't a surprise. The lieutenant scorned Negroes, rarely taking their reports about crime seriously. And while he brutalized many kinds of suspects, he seemed to save the worst treatment for black ones. The great leader booted around the Whites and the Chinese, but he ground his heel into the Blacks.

Oddly, though, it appeared that this racist cop had a dark and forbidden fantasy—Gina. Nobody leered at her more than he did. It was as obvious and ugly as a neglected boil. And perhaps I undermined his fantasy when I started openly dating her. I immediately went from being someone he disliked to someone he abhorred. My long-term career prospects in the bureau plummeted, which would have been terrible only if I had actually liked working at that crazy place. I soon left there to remake myself into a different kind of dick, a private one who set and followed his own rules.

Gina and I grew ever closer over the next year, and that fact scared the Hell out of me. As much as I cared for her, being in love still seemed like something foreign, some import from an imaginary land far, far away. At the least, it was impractical. I convinced myself that being a good gumshoe required me to sleep with clients and contacts; it led to a freer flow of information and greater payoffs. Was sleeping on the job fair to Gina, especially if she would become my wife? I explained all that to her, and she was crushed. But she hinted that my kiss-off was hiding something, that I was actually ending the relationship in part because of race. Her idea sounded wrong, but I couldn't completely argue it away.

One thing I knew: I wasn't discriminating against Gina because of her skin color. Long before I ever met her, I was convinced that Negroes had gotten the rawest of deals in the so-called Free World, the Land of Liberty. They were kidnapped from their homelands, chained into ships sailing for the United States, and then sold as slaves in the South. The Civil War was later fought to free them, but true freedom for blacks never really emerged, certainly not in the South, but not in the rest of the country either. Freedom was limited, and mistreatment was rampant. Their continued plight sometimes gave me a kind of nausea.

But I realized that if I stayed with Gina, race would become my own personal problem. I'd have to constantly worry about the treatment of my black wife and my black children. I didn't even know if I had it in me to be a good husband and father. But I knew for sure I wasn't a social worker. I wasn't a social activist. I wasn't a politician. I wasn't even a voter. I couldn't change bad or unfair behavior. I was a dick—and an incredibly selfish and self-sufficient one at that. Gina was apparently right: Race did impact my thinking.

Unfortunately, the breakup didn't spell the end credits for our relationship. I missed her like you miss a lost hand or eye; you never find anything that can replace it. Then a perplexing case—my last one in San Francisco—gave me the excuse to reach out to her again. I was looking for a rich client's missing sister, and I had only one lead: the murder of a different-named woman who looked exactly like her. I called Gina for the inside file on this killing, and Fate seemed to deal me a pair of aces: The file helped prove the murder victim to be my client's sister, and the call helped reignite our relationship.

Soon, though, I discovered that I had read the cards wrong. In solving the client sister's murder, I also uncovered the existence of an assassination ring, manned by organized crime and the detective bureau, and headed by the mayor and the police chief. Before I could do anything about that information, several members of the ring kidnapped Gina and I and prepared to wipe us out. I felt like I was counting out the remaining minutes of our lives, but the truth was that you couldn't ever count on anything—even the worst. Another one of my clients, an amnesiac whose memory I had helped restore, showed up and wiped out our captors. He was a member of their ring and, in fact, had been the hit man on the sister's murder. But he felt he owed me something and paid me back by playing the unlikely hero. I couldn't even be the hero in my own crazy case.

With how much we knew about local corruption and the personalities involved, Gina and I couldn't safely remain in the Bay Area. I persuaded her to leave with me to the City of the Angels. But our near-death experience and my large role in bringing it about had spooked her—the morning now feared that the nighttime could always decide to shut things down early. When she approached me with a teary voice and a determined look, I knew I was in trouble.

"Matt, I want to enjoy a long life with you. But how can I count on that when you're running around all day and night with desperate and dangerous people? I'm not naïve about the world—I know it's troubled. But why do you have to make a living putting yourself—and potentially, your loved ones—in the dead middle of all that trouble? I'm sorry Matt, but I just can't be your wife or even your girlfriend as long as you remain a private detective."

Her announcement left me with an ache that I couldn't trace to any physical location. And it hurt worse than any pain I had ever experienced before. The reasoning behind her decision also made me angry and defiant, and it was those feelings that dominated my thinking.

"Gina, be realistic, what am I supposed to do if I don't work as a dick? All of my experience has been in the dark arts—assassinating the enemy for the U.S. Army, crooking the law as a San Francisco cop in a suit, sorting through clients' dirty laundry as a dick for hire. I don't know how to do anything else. Maybe you want me to be a librarian sorting books and stamping library cards? A businessman selling people stuff they don't need?"

"Matt, you're a college graduate. From the University of Chicago, of all places. There are a lot of things you can do."

"Yes, I'm a college graduate—and qualified to do nothing. That is what's waiting for me somewhere over the rainbow: Nothing."

She looked down at the floor and said...nothing.

"Sweetheart, I love you and dearly want to be with you. But if you're going to slap conditions on me, I'll have to move on." I was being firm—in a beseeching tone. "Do you really want to give up on us because of what I do for a living?" Gina stayed silent. She wasn't going to budge. She was being as defiant as I was. It was a battle of wills—or actually, will nots. So I finally just leaned forward, kissed her softly, and walked out. That was the last time I saw her.

CHAPTER FOUR

But reviewing that past didn't answer the question that really nagged at me: How did Rose Fischetti find out about Gina?

Chapter Five

"And that's very important to me, Mr. Moulton… Mr.
Moulton?… Mr. Moulton?"

"Oh yes, Mrs. Fischetti?"

"It seemed as if you weren't listening."

"I apologize. I drifted off into deep thought for a few seconds.
Do you mind if I smoke?"

"No, please, go right ahead."

I offered her a cigarette, but she declined.

Once I lit my smoke, I was ready for client business again.
"Mrs. Fischetti, how did you know that I had a black girlfriend?"

She leaned farther back in her chair, like a judge ready to
pronounce a sentence. "When I decided to use a detective to
search for Julie, I wanted to make sure I hired the very best
person, or as close to the best person as I could get. So I sent
my attorney to Los Angeles to conduct a manhunt. He fully
investigated several detectives, several really good dicks, and
found out every last thing he could about them. Every. Last.
Thing.

"We finally settled on you, based in part on your personal
qualities."

"I didn't know I had any of those." What she told me made

me very uncomfortable. The problem wasn't that she found out about Gina. My real concern was that I was supposed to be the one investigating people; people weren't supposed to be investigating me. I hated the idea of being some other snoop's target.

"You have a charming sense of humor, Mr. Moulton. But I consider the search for Julie to be a very serious matter." It sounded a little as if she was scolding me. "She's my only child...."

"Of course, Mrs. Fischetti. Your daughter's very dear to you—I understand that. I was just marveling at your misplaced confidence in the sweetness of my personality. But sweetness or no, I always dedicate myself to my client's cause. You wouldn't have to worry that I'd bail out on you if things got tough. In this case, I would do so only if I discovered that Julie had been taken by your embittered mob friends. I'm not part of a mob nor do I wish to antagonize one, and so I'd have to draw the line there."

"Understood, Mr. Moulton."

"Well, that's it: I guess I'm your man, Mrs. Fischetti." She conspicuously relaxed, as if she were finally letting out a long-held breath. Her mouth even seemed poised to smile.

"I'll need Julie's last address and phone number in LA. And I want you to tell me a little bit more about Michael. Did he live with anyone here in Chicago? Does he have a family? Do you have an address and phone number for his relatives?"

The subject of Michael never played well on her face—her eyes narrowed, her lips tightened, and her cheeks puckered as if she was biting into the sourest lemon. But she surely knew that a dick, like an attorney, lived off facts; they were his air and water. "He stayed with his father. His mother had died long ago, when he was a small child." She took a pen and pad from the drawer.

"Where is your attorney?"

"He's still in LA, doing work for the organization."

"On your piece of paper, write down his name and number, and a number at which I can reach you directly. I'm sorry to put you through all this hard labor, Mrs. Fischetti," I said, with an irony I hoped she wouldn't catch.

"I'd write out a book of names and numbers if it would help you find Julie. I'm...I'm grateful that you accepted this job. I'll pay you anything you ask when you find her."

"No, that's all right, Mrs. Fischetti, we already have a deal—a thousand now and a thousand later. I can easily live with that." I stood up, shook her hand, and asked her if the butler would call me a cab. "I'll be in touch," I said, as I finally left her stuffy and oppressive office. An hour in the presence of so much power was more than enough for me.

I was accustomed to working in a fog, but nothing like the one that obscured Chicago that afternoon. The aggressive drizzle turned into an antagonistic mist, daring the cabbie to drive down streets we could barely see. It was the city's version of light precipitation.

We were trying to head to a neighborhood deeper into the city's South Side. In physical distance, it was close to the black, aspiringly middle-class Bronzeville and the white, largely upper-class Hyde Park. But by any other measurement, this black neighborhood on the busy concrete of State Street existed far, far away. The cabbie left me at my address, a blocky, disheveled, and badly aging three-story apartment building that sat between a run-down tavern on one side and an abandoned storefront on the other. A few nearby homes seemed almost shanty-like. Yet you still couldn't label this neighborhood a "slum"—it rose above that. It looked more like some of the declining working-class neighborhoods, mainly black but some white, that I had dicked through in LA and San Francisco. It teetered and wheezed its way to something approaching a tough-skinned, still dignified survival.

The building's paint-flaked outer hall greeted me with a wall of labeled mailboxes. I looked for the one that said William Sykes, home of Michael's father. I pressed the doorbell, and in a minute that passed like an hour, William finally rang me back. He lived at the end of the first floor, just past the apartment reeking of hot grease and the apartment resounding with a couple heatedly exchanging views. I knocked on the door and heard a modulated voice droning on behind it. A medium-tall black man with coiled, light-gray hair opened the door and didn't seem happy about it.

"Yes?"

"Pardon me, pal, I'm looking for William Sykes. My name is Matt Moulton, and I'm a private detective."

"I'm William Sykes, but what would a private dick want with me?"

"I'm really looking for information about your son, Michael. May I come in for a few minutes, Mr. Sykes?"

The mention of Michael apparently made me more acceptable to him. "Come in, please. Have a seat." He immediately went to the new television set and lowered its volume and then—thinking better of it—shut the thing off.

The place was an organized mess. Rolled-up magazines, open beers, half-eaten snacks, and recently removed shirts and jackets were strewn over the living room—exactly where they could be found when needed. His organizational style strongly

43

suggested that no people of the female persuasion lived there.

"Would you like a beer?"

"Oh, yes, thank you." He brought back a can from the kitchen, opened it, and handed it to me.

"Your name again was…Moulton?"

"Yes."

"Well, Mr. Moulton, you're lucky because I'm ordinarily working at the plant right now. I got sick late this morning and had to come home early."

"What kind of work do you do?"

"I bottle sodas—grape, orange, root beer, crème. It's tedious work, but it's a union job, paying better than anything I've done since the end of the war. And I get to drink as much crème soda as I want." He grinned at the thought.

It was hard to place William chronologically. The long, deep creases in his cheeks and the purplish pits under his eyes suggested that he was older. But his upright posture and rock-solid build made him look younger. I split the difference, guessing he was somewhere just over 50.

"Mr. Sykes, do you keep in contact with Michael? I ask because Rose Fischetti hired me to find her daughter, Julie, who disappeared in Los Angeles more than two months ago. Julie and Michael had been living together just before that happened."

He shook his head and raised his voice. "Oh, the Fischetti women? They're much more trouble than they're worth." He took a gulp of his bitter beer and then wiped his mouth with his t-shirt's sleeve. "That Julie lured him all the way out to Hollywood, where they struggled for two years with little or no work. Michael finally became fed up with the stars business and tried persuading her to return to Chicago with him. She just wouldn't go, and then one day she walked out on him."

"Was that last August?"

"Ah, yes, I believe so. Mike wrote me right after it happened."

"Did he know where she went?"

"Yes, and he decided to stay in LA and keep working on her to go back. He insists that he'll be able to change her mind. Ha!" He slapped his knee with contempt.

"Do you know her new address?"

"No, I'd have to ask Michael for it."

"Did he move from their apartment?"

"Yes, her mother's checks had been paying for part of their pricey rent. And so he had to move. He rented a cheaper place and shares it with another guy."

"He has a job, I presume."

"Yes, he works as a pianist at the Blue Way Inn in his neighborhood of South Los Angeles. But I'm telling you, Mr. Moulton: He's wasting his life chasing after that rich, spoiled brat. That boy has stars in his eyes, and it's blinding him."

"You may be right, Mr. Sykes. Beauty and the beast have led him astray."

"Beauty and the beast?"

"Yes, the Fischetti beauty and the Hollywood beast. A young man with an ego wants to conquer both. Good luck with that."

"You're a smart dick, Mr. Moulton."

"Smart? I don't know if that's the right word to describe me. Try weary, wary, and worn—it's a combination that keeps me out of trouble, most of the time. Meanwhile, if you'll give me Michael's address, I'll shove off and leave you to your TV programs."

"Oh, right," he said with a distracted look in his deep-set eyes. The tube seemed to be the furthest thing from his mind right now. "Mr. Moulton, do let me know if Michael gets into any trouble."

"Sure thing, Mr. Sykes. I appreciate your help." He almost seemed sorry to see me go.

Now I was desperate to find a good bar with a real drink and a working phone booth. I needed to call Sara with the latest news about the case. And I wanted to send her off in a new direction with her research—Viogram Pictures. I had the vague feeling that something wasn't quite right there, but the only way I could resolve or flesh out the idea was with more dope about how the place operated.

After the call and after the drink (or three), I planned to spend the rest of my Chicago time with mom and dad. I was certain that they would be happy to see their overworked and under-accomplished man boy.

Chapter Six

After I returned to LA and got a stationary night's sleep, I immediately set out for Michael Syke's apartment. Michael held the key to a quick resolution of the missing Julie case. With his info, I could find her, talk to her, and—at the very least—encourage her to call home. I would even pay the toll.

I drove South on the busy Alameda thoroughfare, ultimately turning down a narrow, nondescript side street. Michael's building was a flimsy, old, two-story frame house that seemed to have the shakes, the result of the furiously vibrating train traveling the nearby tracks. I suddenly couldn't get away from the railroad. But people in this working-class, semi-industrial neighborhood lived with its motion and commotion every single day—train after train after train. It undoubtedly wearied them while literally wearing away the places they called home. The train was a permanent resident, a forever intruding neighbor. But how could they complain? The sun was always shining, and there was always a paycheck—from one job or another—waiting for them every Friday afternoon. It constituted the alleged LA paradise.

I walked up the stairs to the building's small, ramshackle wooden porch. What looked like two kitchen chairs provided outside seating near the building's single door, to the right of which hung two labeled mailboxes. One said Sykes/Sullivan 2; I pressed the doorbell underneath it. There was no response, and so I pressed it again and again. Then I tried ringing the other bell, for the first-floor apartment. What a surprise: No one was home during the late morning of a workday. Heading down the stairs, I suddenly encountered a young Negro man on his weary way up. He sported a bruise under his left eye and a tired, vacant look that suggested a night of missed sleep. His casual clothes stuck to him like an outer skin—a moist and shriveled one ready for shedding.

"Excuse me, are you Michael Sykes?"

"No, I'm not." He swallowed hard and looked down at the old porch floor. "Michael is no longer with us. He was murdered last night."

I was used to getting bad news, hearing about death, and other terrible things. But my long experience with the worst didn't make it any easier to manage and accept this revelation. I felt as if someone had just plunged a battering ram into my gut. As I was trying to get my wind back, I thought of the young life lost and what that might mean about Julie Fischetti and my increasingly complicated case.

"What happened? How and where was he murdered?" The Mob immediately broke into my thoughts.

"Michael was apparently beaten to death. It happened yesterday in our apartment upstairs." He was still gulping with the fact. "Who are you?"

"I'm sorry. I'm Matt Moulton, a private investigator. I was hired to find Julie Fischetti, Michael's girlfriend. Her mother stopped hearing from her and was concerned about her well-being and safety. And you are Michael's roommate? What's your name?"

"The name is Richard Sullivan."

"Mr. Sullivan, would you invite me upstairs where we can talk further about all this?"

His body slightly withdrew. He didn't seem enthusiastic about the idea. It was as if I were offering to show him my emerging smallpox infection. But he relented, and we trudged upstairs.

The apartment was minimally furnished. There were a couple of ragged easy chairs, a couple of worn throw rugs, and a radio and phonograph. A kitchen, a bathroom, and two bedrooms with mattresses on the floor completed the layout. Murder took up the most space, with large blood spots on the floor and more blood splattered all over a living room wall. The place was once home sweet home, but now it was a violent crime scene.

We finally sat down. "Mr. Moulton, please excuse my reluctance to invite you up here. But I've just experienced the worst night of my life. After a long day at work and then a double date at the movies, I came home and found poor Michael dead, beaten to a bloody pulp. His face was swollen and disfigured…. He was almost unrecognizable." You could almost see that sight in his frightened eyes.

"I immediately called the police. But when they got here, they started acting like I killed him. I mean…what the fuck? Why would I kill my friend and roommate and then report it to the police? They took me in for questioning and kept me in their office all night and into this morning. They threw one question after another at me, and when they didn't like my answer, they'd get rough and twist my ear, pull my hair, slap and even slug me." He winced and sighed. His battle-weary face seemed to want to go into hiding. "After all that, I haven't slept for more than thirty hours. So I'm sorry, Mr. Moulton, I'm in bad shape." His eyes were shot blood-red.

"Who was the detective in charge of your...interrogation?"

"It was a lieutenant, a big guy by the name of Brad Pascal." Even just repeating the name seemed to make him flinch.

"Oh yeah, I know him well. He can sometimes be almost reasonable. But—in the end—he's probably too much like a lot of other detectives. They want to solve everything yesterday. And if you're an ordinary guy, particularly if you're Black, you're guilty until proven innocent in their eyes. Now, if you have money and influence, that's an entirely different story...." I wasn't certain if he heard my last words because another train had just come rustling and whistling through.

"This guy, Pascal, oversaw everything, but even he got tired and needed sleep. He went home, but my grilling continued."

"Did you offer them witnesses to confirm your alibi?

"Oh, yes. I told them I went out with three people from work. I kept repeating my friends' names and giving them the names of my supervisor and other co-workers. I even furnished them with the name of the movie theater we went to and the movie we saw. But the cops wouldn't listen to me. Finally, after hours and hours of questioning, they decided to contact my witnesses this morning." He still seemed amazed by it all, and that told me that he hadn't had much previous experience with the LA police.

"What movie did you see?" I asked out of sheer curiosity.

"Sunset Boulevard."

I shook my head wearily. It somehow seemed horribly apt that last night he should go see a fatally dark film about Michael and Julie's Hollywood.

50

"Where do you work?"

"Not far from here. I work in a big plant that specializes in making picture tubes and other television parts. But, after my employer found out about this encounter with the police, I worry that I won't have that job much longer."

"So you worked the day shift, and Michael worked the night? Did you ever get the chance to go out with him and Julie?"

That question momentarily stumped him, as if I was asking him about meetings with Franklin and Eleanor Roosevelt. "Actually, I never met Julie. But Michael talked about her all the time. He was so proud of her accomplishments in pictures. But he was also worried about her because she was supposedly involved in something that might have been dangerous. But he was never specific about what that was."

"Did she work?"

"Yes, but I don't know where."

"And would he regularly go visit her?"

"Yes, but I don't know where she lived or where they'd go. Despite all his talk about Julie, I actually learned very little about her. She was a mystery, and that's why I sometimes wondered if she really existed, outside those movies, of course."

"Did Michael keep an address book?"

"I don't know, but you can check his room."

Beside the isolated mattress, Michael's space contained a small chest of drawers. It was bright red, and it was the room's one indulgence. Shaving materials and cosmetics topped the chest, while t-shirts, underwear, and various other personal items—including studio publicity photos—filled the drawers. I opened the drawers with a towel to avoid leaving my prints. But there was no address book. The only thing of potential value I found was a small rubber-banded stack of photos starring Julie and Michael. Some of the pictures were shot in an attractive apartment. Was it Julie's current place, Michael and Julie's former apartment, or someplace else? I took a couple of the photos with me.

By the time I returned to the living room, Richard Sullivan's now puffy eyelids were lowering to half-mast. Once sleep fully overtook him, I guessed that he'd be knocked out until tomorrow morning, barring—of course—another visit from the police. "I'm sorry about your last twelve hours," I said in a kind of hard whisper. We shook hands. "I wish you much better luck for the next twelve." He didn't look very hopeful. Another train stormed through as I quietly headed out the door.

Michael Sykes's death changed my travel plans—I now had to drive downtown to the detective bureau and see if I could find Lieutenant Pascal. It was only hours ago he apparently went home. But I wouldn't have been surprised if he had already returned to the office. The man didn't seem to have a life outside the LA police force. Yes, he did have a wife, but she was more of a necessary inconvenience than a life partner. Solving crimes was his true life, and that would have been narrow-mindedly fine but for one fact: No one gave more effort to less effect than Pascal. He wasn't stupid or incompetent; he just made a lot of bad decisions. Still, he knew a lot, and it was important for someone like me—a dick always looking for the missing details—to check in with him now and again.

If I had arrived at the bureau's set of offices blindfolded, I would have been able to identify the place immediately. It had a distinct odor, smelling of cigarette smoke, burnt coffee, mildewed paper, and years-old sweat, with a slight trace of urine. The last smell emanated from the ladies' room directly across the hall; its outer door didn't completely close, and the cleaning help apparently didn't overwork themselves overusing the detergent. Air conditioning would have mitigated, if not eliminated, the problem, but the city government couldn't afford it. Besides, where was the corruption potential in air conditioning?

When I walked in, Mabel Banks, the departmental secretary, greeted me with an impatient grin. She was a grandmotherly woman with her gray hair rolled in a bun and her sensible gray dress buttoned up to the neckline. At least that was the way she looked. The way she acted and sounded, however, suggested someone more in the line of a combination failed comedian and reformed convict.

"Hey, Moulton, what brings you and your long face into our office today?"

"I had some time on my hands, and I thought I'd spend it with you."

"If you've come specially to see me, you're not only as crazy as they say you are, but you're also some kind of a nasty pervert."

"Okay then, let me turn myself in to Pascal. Is he in the office?"

"What do you think? Isn't he always here? The question is whether he wants to bother with you right now or ever. Don't hold your breath, Don Juan, but let me check."

A half-minute later, Madame Insult returned. "Go right in: His majesty will see you now."

"Thanks, Mabel, it's been charming," I said, doffing my beige fedora.

I entered Pascal's office and found that everything was still there—the large desk with cigarette butts spilling out of the ashtray and coffee stains caked and hardened near his center drawer, too many chairs haphazardly arranged around the room, and the small, always unoccupied desk sitting in the corner, where he kept piles of files. All that was missing was Pascal himself, and so I just took a seat and waited, listening to the birds on the ledge just outside the open window. It sounded like they were complaining about big city life.

"Hi Matt, good to see you." An unjacketed Pascal bounded into the room with a cigarette in his mouth, a couple of files in one hand, and a cup of no doubt cold coffee in the other. He always carried the cup around, spilled parts of it here and there, brought it up to his mouth, but never seemed to drink from it. He didn't offer me his hand to shake.

"What brings you in today?" His unshaven, chubby-cheeked, forty-five-year-old face displayed an affable suspiciousness. In his mind, everybody was hiding something, and he was going to find out what that was—even if you weren't a suspect. He pulled on his already loosened blue tie.

"Lieutenant, I wanted to talk about the Michael Sykes case."

He raised the dark bushes above his eyes. "Oh?... Sykes? What's your connection to him? A client case of yours?" He poked and twisted his half-finished cigarette into the ashtray and lighted a fresh one.

"Yes, there's a connection."

"Well, what is it? Who's your client?"

"Lieutenant, I didn't come here to be grilled. And you know that client information is confidential—you can't force it from me."

"Look, Matt, I've always cut you a lot of slack. But if I begin to suspect that you're covering up for someone connected to murder...."

"Where's that insider's insight of yours? Don't you know by

now that I don't cover up murders or obstruct investigations? I'm just asking you for a little information, stuff that's about to become public or may become public under the right conditions."

He looked down at his desk and repetitively puffed away on his new cigarette. Studying his now thoughtful face, I started thinking about unfairness, the large and the small of it. The large may have felled Sykes last night. But the small has victimized Pascal. Life had left him with too much hair in his brows and too little hair on his head. The imbalance has undermined his authority by making him look a little ridiculous, like a comedy figure. Did he then try to overcompensate himself by being more authoritarian and even more brutal? Life was a freakish affair.

"Okay, Matt, the results of the medical examination and other evidence we've collected suggest that the murderer may not have initially intended to kill Sykes. He wanted something from him, like information or silence, and Sykes apparently refused to deliver. The perpetrator kept trying to change his mind, but the beating finally went too far."

"You say perpetrator. Couldn't it have been more than one?" The Mob likes to work in twos.

"No, the medical examiner thinks it was one man."

"It was an especially brutal beating?"

"Oh, yes. I haven't seen a beating this savage in a while." He nervously began puffing on that idea.

"To inflict that kind of damage, the murderer must have been a huge man, correct? Why then did you guys spend so much time and effort interrogating Richard Sullivan, who's not only a slightly built man but also someone with a verifiable alibi?"

He fumed and snuffed out his smoke in the tray. "Who are

you, Sullivan's attorney? We were looking for information—we didn't know then what we know now. Matt, don't tell me how to do my job."

"I'm not. I just want to make sure I wasn't missing something. Why focus on Sullivan, a Sykes friend and roommate? Is it because he's a Negro?"

Pascal banged his hand on the desk, which shook the cup and spilled more of his coffee. "Oh, no, are you going to turn my questioning into a racial issue? Color had nothing to do with how I approached Sullivan. Stop trying to be so noble, Matt. Who are you, the White Knight?"

I laughed. "Not at all, Brad. All I'm trying to say is this: Even if you don't care about fairness, I would imagine you'd be very concerned about success." The anger in his eyes started to dissipate. "You know better than anyone else that it's hard to solve a murder. But it becomes near impossible if you're pursuing the wrong people as suspects. Now you certainly don't have to listen to me. I'm just a gumshoe with unhappy experience as a public dick. I'm always stumbling around in the dark, but I'm also forever reminding myself that I'll never find the right path—the path of light—if I keep my eyes closed and my mind made up."

Pascal still wasn't happy with me, but his silence told me that he recognized the truth of what I said. He shook his head and lit another cigarette.

I stood up. "But I appreciate the info, Lieutenant. Every little bit helps."

"Yeah, yeah. The best way to thank me is to pay me back—call when you get any leads. I'll expect to hear from you."

"You're always on my mind, lieutenant. S'long!"

Chapter Seven

While I had just started chasing down the missing Julie, I already felt as if I was running out of time. The fear preyed on my mind as I returned to the office that afternoon, for the first time in days. Sara was on the phone, taking and typing notes. And so I repaired to my inner office to pour a drink, light a smoke, and start a debate with myself about what to do next. It was my first of the day for each one, and together they provided a much-needed form of succor and security. From where could I draw a lead on Julie—The police? Organized crime? Hollywood business? The police wouldn't know. Organized crime wouldn't tell. And that left only business—the one called Viogram, Julie's studio. They might be in a position to know and tell, and that's why I looked forward to Sara's report.

As if she was reading my mind, Sara soon hurried into my office with papers in her hands. She was dressed in her green jacket-and-skirt outfit, but without the jacket this time. The weather was too warm, and she was too busy to stand on formalities. She had the right idea, and so I removed my jacket as well.

"Welcome home, Matt. How was Chicago?" She sat down in my client chair.

"It was another town—one with probably too many personal memories attached. Otherwise, as I told you, the Fischetti and Sykes interviews proved fruitful. But now I'm going to impose upon you with something unpleasant—I want you to phone Sykes. You need to break the news to him that his son is dead."

"Oh, no! What happened?" The blood seemed to leave her face.

"Michael was beaten to death last night in his apartment."

"My God! Do they know who did it?"

"Of course not. Pascal tried to pin it on Michael's black roommate, but that didn't stick. And so now he and his bureau are acting lost."

"Who do you think did it—the Mob?"

My gut wanted to say yes. "The Mob is the obvious answer, but maybe that's a little too easy. The past is warning me to think complicated—or at least head in that direction. For now, I'm more interested in learning about Viogram. At the very least, they should be able to tell us a lot more about Julie. So waddya got, sweetheart?"

She stood up, started walking around, and looking through her papers. Sara had now retreated to another world. "Well, Matt, Viogram is a small studio that stands out by making anonymous pictures. The place churns out the lowest of the so-called "B" movies, the quick, inexpensive features that play on the second half of double bills. They do a lot of action adventures, crime films, and race pictures. But again, most of them are cheaply made and lack the big stars of big-studio films. They tell their stories with over-the-hill actors and young, would-be players like Julie and Michael.

"This new kind of studio was the brainchild of a rich guy by the name of George Frederick Baines, who had made his wealth hustling new products and inventions during the post-World War I economic boom. He started Viogram Pictures in 1927, and it really thrived, particularly during the 30s; people seemed to find its fare entertaining. The studio got an economic boost when Baines married Ruth Gettling in 1932."

I had to bring Sara back. "Gettling of the Gettling Steel fortune? Didn't her father die and leave her everything?"

"Yes, all his money and all his stock in Gettling Steel, which had gone public in the 20s."

"How old was she when she married Baines?"

"She was 22. He was 42."

I couldn't help grinning. "He wanted to be her mentor, I guess. With a fortune like that, he could have mentored her into turning Viogram into two Metro Goldwyn Mayers."

"Yes, for years, the press speculated that Baines would use his wife's wealth to at least upgrade the studio product—start making better 'B' and even some high-class 'A' pictures, a combo for which RKO Pictures became famous. But that never happened during Baines' reign. Ruth's money, which she continued to control, went to helping Viogram stick to its aggressively modest ways."

"Turning out the penny candy of pictures?"

Sara smiled. "Yes, but even doing just that became more of a challenge in the early 1940s. Baines got terribly sick with diabetes, a severe blood sugar disorder. He slowed down and proved unable to respond to the changing Hollywood product during the war years. The bigger studios were giving racy "B" plots the "A" treatment and also creating more films in color. How then does a little studio like Viogram compete as profitably as before? People close to Baines were advising him to take the company public so that it could more easily raise money for better pictures. But he refused, resolving to keep the company under his faltering private control. You want my view? I think he coveted more of his wife's money for the studio. However, death had the final word on everything. In 1945, Baines succumbed to a diabetes attack."

I lit another smoke and drew hard. "When people were pushing Baines to go corporate, where did wife Ruthie stand on that issue?"

Sara flipped through her papers. "Oh, I don't believe I found out her initial view about that. However, after her husband died, Ruth took Viogram public, and she became the Chairman of the Board of Directors for the new corporation. Viogram, Inc. soon established a division called Creative Artists, which would make occasional higher-budget, higher-quality films. It also introduced something called Entertainment Services, a pure profit center, which would produce and sell such things as drug-store paperback versions of some of its movies. By all accounts, going public boosted Viagram's bottom line."

"If Ruth oversees the whole operation as the Chairman of the Board, who actually runs Viogram on a day-to-day basis? I guess the person I'm asking about is the Chief Executive Officer."

"Yes, that would be Spencer Morgan: He's the actual company head. Before Viogram, he never worked in Hollywood. He specialized in corporate administration and governance at a couple of companies. He's a completely different kind of leader than Baines was—more bureaucratic and behind the scenes. He's not really a movie man."

I poured myself a short drink. "But who is this guy, Morgan? How did he get the job? How old is he? Was he previously connected to Baines or his wife or maybe both?"

"Yes, by all accounts, he knew both well."

"But do we know if he was closer to Baines or to Ruth?"

"Matt, I see where you're going with that question, but I don't have much information about it. That might be something we can discover only through dicking around. As to your other questions, the Board appointed Morgan the corporate chief. He was 40 at the time."

"So he was essentially appointed by Chairman Ruth?"

"Yes, essentially."

As Sara sat back down, I tried to peer through the lingering smoke. I saw no glamour, only the stuff of business—profit centers and bottom lines and corporate politics and who knows what else. Business was Hollywood's dirty little secret.

"Thanks sweetheart, your report gives me wonderful insight into the place and the people. Is there anything you want to add?"

"You know, pulling back the curtain on Viogram is going to ruin my appreciation of movies. Knowing too much almost kills the fantasy," she said, with a kind of ironic sigh.

"There's no more escape. By that, I mean escape from the inevitable: You have to call Sykes now." She let out a sad laugh. "And please follow up with Pascal by encouraging him to do the same, and give Michael's father the whole story. The lieutenant needs to infer that my future cooperation depends on his doing his job."

"I'll tell him that without saying it."

"Thank you, dear!"

I had a lot more to do that afternoon. I called Viogram to set up an appointment with someone who could give me the dope on current contract players. The Public Relations Director would see me tomorrow morning. I never had public relations before.

I also needed to perform some of my own pre-research—touch documents, read stories, and talk to people. So I scoured the library, looked at some publicly available city files, exchanged ideas with a couple of Hollywood press insiders, and—finally—called on one of my favorite people: the county medical examiner. No one knew more about the way people live and die. I was now ready for Viogram.

Chapter Eight

The next morning, I went to Sunset Boulevard—the street, not the movie. With an address in the forty hundreds, Viogram studio occupied almost five acres of space, and yet that somehow seemed disappointing and inadequate. If studios such as Metro Goldwyn Mayer and Paramount resembled sprawling small towns, Viogram looked more like one of their neighborhoods—one of the smaller ones. Just beyond the guards at the studio gate, a horizontally compact, two-story, orange-brick building greeted visitors and workers with all the company's offices. That was it—that was Viogram. The whole layout suggested pinched space, tight money, and small-scale—moviemaking as a cheap magical trick. Did a long box and a white-tipped wand make Julie disappear?

The lobby and offices presented an entirely different view. Everything was remodeled and new. But it was a vague kind of new, a corporate-style modern. The feel was highly sanitized, as if the purpose was to convey a cheerful efficiency and profitability, but nothing else. There were no signs of the corporation's actual work. In fact, I didn't spot a single picture or painting anywhere—that would have been too distracting. If I hadn't known where I was, I would never have guessed that I was in the offices of a movie studio. The place seemed to incorporate the postwar American approach to business, the total pursuit of the corporate ideal—impersonal power. Meanwhile, there was still no air conditioning.

The Public Relations Department lay just off the lobby. It was full of important-seeming people rushing here and there, popping into this office and popping out of that one, with thick files and loose papers in their hands. I needed to find somebody—anybody—who was sitting or standing still. That person occupied a sizable desk that sat in front of the end office. She was young, probably just out of some kind of school, perhaps college. She had big cheeks, little eyes, an authentic smile, and a very pleasing and helpful manner.

"May I help you, sir? You seem lost."

"Well, that's nothing new. In this case, I'm looking for Bob Rosen. I have an appointment with him. My name is Matt Moulton."

"Oh yes, Mr. Moulton, please have a seat. I'll let him know you're here. Would you like a cup of coffee?"

"No thanks, I've had too much already."

Before I could make myself comfortable in the waiting area, she came back out to lead me into the boss man's office. The second I walked through the door, Director Rosen plunged after me with his hand out and his smile on. He was about 35 years young, wore a light beige suit on a tall and rangy frame, and sported round eyeglasses with transparent frames.

"Good morning, Mr. Moulton. It's nice to see you. Thank you for stopping by today. Please sit down." He acted as if my appearance made his day.

"Mr. Rosen, I'm a private investigator looking for a missing woman who has been a part of your company. Her name is

Julie Fischetti."

He somehow managed to frown while retaining his smile. "Oh, that's too bad. I'm sorry for your difficulty. Now, how can I help you?"

I wondered if this was an act or if he really was that dense. "You can help by telling me whether she still works here and by giving me the most recent address you have for her."

"Oh yes, of course. You need information. We try to do what we can to serve the public." He went silent.

"Well, I'm part of the public. I've even seen a Viogram picture or two. Now, how about serving me with some dope on Julie Fischetti?"

"Yes, I see. But we face a challenge here." His smile almost disappeared. "Sharing private information isn't part of my task set. I represent public relations—I relate to our public."

"Oh, I understand, pal. You don't help, you relate. Well, who does help? Where can I get this information?"

"You would need to go to our Human Resources Department."

I shook my head and laughed. "Human Resources, you say?"

Why not Personnel? Why not the Employee Department? The term Human Resources was worthless corporate jargon. In fact, it was insidious because it worked to depersonalize. It turned people into things, materials, tools—mere Human resources. But I couldn't let that distract me. Again, I wasn't a social critic—I was a dick on a missing person's case.

"Okay, okay, can you get me an appointment with the head of Human Resources?"

"I most certainly will, Mr. Moulton." He picked up the phone and called someone. As I waited, I wondered if it would have been easier to deal with gangsters. They were more dangerous but much easier to understand. As I pondered that thought, I lit a cigarette. It helped me to concentrate.

Before I could get very far with that, my public relator came back. "I've set you up to see Gregory McClintock, the Director of Human Resources. His office is on the Northeast corner of the second floor."

"Good work, Mr. Rosen," I said as a taunt. "So long." I left in a puff of smoke.

He called after me: "Thank you, Mr. Moulton. It was a pleasure to serve you. Come see us again sometime...."

Time changes everything. Because it was now lunchtime, the second floor had emptied out. The bees were no longer in the corporate hive. However, I found McClintock's office with McClintock still in it. I knocked on the open door.

"Mr. McClintock?"

"Matt Moulton? Well, come in and take a seat," he said, as if that represented a burden to him.

McClintock's office was exactly the same as Rosen's. It had the same polished wood desk sitting on the same plush brown rug. The small difference was that McClintock kept a bud vase with a striking yellow flower on his desk. I wondered how the corporate police permitted such defiance.

But McClintock was no Rosen. He was a different person with a different job. Unlike Rosen, who answered questions, McClintock asked them—a large part of his job involved grilling people who wanted to join Viogram. Were they the right human resources for the job, for the company? He apparently wrestled with that all the time, and it showed. McClintock was wrinkled: His drawn face was wrinkled, his baggy suit was wrinkled, his whole weary manner was wrinkled. The job—and all the rest of his life—appeared to wear on him like anvils.

"So tell me, Mr. Moulton, what is the nature of your visit here today?"

"I'm a private investigator, and I'm looking for someone—I guess you would call her one of your human resources. She's a young woman by the name of Julie Fischetti."

"And why are you looking for this woman?" His look was cold, and his tone was haughty.

I blew smoke in his face. "Because she's disappeared."

"You say she's an employee of this company?"

"Well, I don't know if she's on the weekly payroll. She's an actress who signed a contract with you people more than two years ago. She then appeared in a couple of your movies. I need to know whether she's doing anything for you right now and whether you can provide an address where I can reach her. It's as simple as that."

"Well, Mr. Moulton, it's not so simple." I thought he was about to tell me that I didn't get the job. "As Director of Human Resources, I oversee employees, not contract players. I have nothing to do with the actors and actresses."

I raised my voice. "And what if she's not a contract player but a current employee? Look, McClintock, you have access to a lot of information. You can spare a couple minutes of your precious time doing a little digging for me. Or aren't you capable of that? Is your problem, as the ads say, 'iron-poor blood?'"

I got the impression that he wasn't accustomed to non-boss people talking to him that way. He looked unhappy about it, but when he tried to dial up some real anger, he soon changed his mind and disconnected the call. His thinking seemed to be: Why antagonize someone like him, who could easily be violent?

"Well, you don't have to get nasty about it, Mr. Moulton. I am a very busy man...."

"Who has nothing else to do right now."

He groaned. "Okay, let me see what I can find out real quick."

He stood up and left his office. I followed him out to the door and watched him go through a big drawer. He removed a file and brought it back to the office and sat down. He seemed proud of himself. "I found her."

He looked through the file but kept it off his desk, away from my prying eyes. "I see a copy of her movie contract. Notes indicate just what you said: she appeared in two movies for us. Let's see....oh, okay, she's still working for Viogram as part of the Entertainment Services Department. I can't tell if she's a contractor or an employee."

"Where does she work and what does she do?"

"Hmmm, that's strange, her file doesn't provide the details. But you could find out that information from the Entertainment Services Department, which is on the other side of this floor. The director's name is Charles Pittman. "

"Okay, would you give me her current address?"

He closed the file. "I'm sorry, Mr. Moulton, I can't divulge such personal information. But maybe Entertainment Services will give it to you. That department has become something of a corporate darling around here, a privileged character," said McClintock, as if he was referring to a resented rival.

That was an interesting tell. The more you talked to people, the more you learned—at least most of the time. But I had had enough of McClintock. "Well, thank you, Mr. McClintock. You've been more of a help—ah, more of a resource—than I expected. Goodbye."

I wandered through the noontime desert until I reached the office of Charles Pittman—who wasn't there. There was a smaller office connected to his, but that was vacant as well. I stood there realizing that I needed a cigarette, a good drink, and an understanding friend. But before I could do anything about it, I felt a sharp poke in my back. I turned around and found myself face to face with a plain-pretty dishwater blonde with irony in her eyes. Despite the seen-it-all expression, she seemed to like what she was looking at right now.

"Well, hello! What can I do for you?"

I could have thought of a million things. After all, she was maturely young (a little over twenty-five), she had striking pale blue eyes, and her body pointed and rounded in all the right ways and directions. But what really appealed to me was her aura—she looked like someone who always ultimately did what she wanted, and you couldn't beat that for sexiness. But my mind was running on one track right now. "You can tell me where I can find Pittman."

"He's out of the office at the moment."

"Is he on the feedbag like everyone else?"

"The feedbag?" She laughed. "Yes, he's at lunch."

"Are you his secretary?"

"No." Her eyes darkened. I had asked the wrong question. "I'm Jeannie Goodwin, his executive assistant. Maybe I can help you."

"My name's Matt—Matt Moulton. I'm a private investigator searching for a missing person, one of your employees or contract actors. Her name is Julie Fischetti."

"Oh…Julie Fischetti?"

"What does 'oh' mean?"

"You need a dictionary? I have one on my desk." She gave

me a million-dollar smile.

"I don't care about Webster's definition. I want to know what you meant by 'oh'"

"Oh well, I meant 'oh, Julie Fischetti.'"

"Do you know her?"

"No, but I know of her."

Authority intruded. "Jeannie, oh Jeannie, I need you to get on the phone with Frank and relay those numbers we talked about this morning," said the man who burst into her office. He came with thick white curls, a flush red face, and an impatient, authoritarian manner.

"Mr. Pittman, this gentleman is waiting to see you. His name is Matt Moulton, a private investigator."

He offered me a reluctant hand. "Greetings, Mr. Molden. I only have a couple minutes to spend with you."

"The name is Moulton."

"Sorry, Moulton. Come right this way." The tall, stoop-shouldered man led me into his office. It was only twice as large as McClintock's and Rosen's offices. Meanwhile, his fine-weave blue pinstripe suit was probably only three times more expensive than his colleagues' businesswear. McClintock was on to something. Companies shouldn't play favorites, but they sure seemed to be doing so with the Entertainment Services Department.

"Now, Mr. Moulton, what's your business here?"

"My business is a missing person who apparently works or once worked for your department. Her name is Julie Fischetti. I need to reach her and make sure she's all right."

He had a face without expression. My mention of Fischetti didn't change a thing—he didn't even blink. Unfortunately, I didn't have any experience reading a bust. "But you're not a real detective. If this person is really missing, why aren't the police involved?"

"My client wants to keep this a private matter for now."

"There's nothing I can do for you, Moulton. I can't just pass out private information about employees to any Tom, Dick, or Harry who walks in the place. "

"So you're confirming that Julie Fischetti is a current, living, breathing employee?"

"I'm not confirming anything—I just can't help you."

"You mean you just won't help me. Pittman, tell me something, why is an apparently respectable public corporation so determined to hide information about one of its employees, a person who may be in real danger right now?"

His top lip made a move to curl, as if his face was about to rebel. But nothing came of it. His face said nothing more, and he stayed silent.

I stood up, raised my voice, and pointed my finger at him. "A minute ago, you said I wasn't real. But you were wrong, Pittman. I'm a dick who can be a real pain in your ass. A bloody pain. I know police, I know press people, and I can easily get them excited about this case and your reaction to it. So if you don't think you'd want to face that kind of heat, that kind of bad publicity, you might consider giving me a call sometime—soon." I took out my business card and threw it in his face. He still didn't blink. His lack of visible anger further infuriated me, and I stalked out.

I couldn't get to the elevator fast enough. After just a year here, I was already tired of Hollywood—or at least Viogram's corporate version of it. I got into the elevator car and pressed floor one, but before the door closed, Jeannie Goodwin slipped in.

"You left so suddenly."

"Blame it on your boss: He doesn't play well with others."

We stepped out of the elevator and headed for the lobby. Her playful look turned thoughtful. "I'd like to talk to you about something. Could we get together at a private bar someplace after work?"

"Sure. Would this be for business or pleasure?"

"Well, let's call it a meeting for the pleasure of business."

"It sounds like an appealing mix. Are you familiar with the Light Way Inn on Wilshire?"

"Oh yeah, I've been there! It's a dark place that Hollywood types haven't discovered yet."

"Hey you get around…to good places. Can you show up at seven?"

"Even better, I can show up at six."

"I'll be there waiting. Bring your candor."

She smiled like a charming know-it-all and hurried back to her office.

I sensed that the case was taking a turn, but—of course—to where was the big question.

Chapter Nine

I sat in the Light Way Inn nursing a scotch and water, and drinking in the atmosphere. The place occupied a rugged basement space with tables and a few booths, smartly dim lighting, scribbled names and phrases on the walls, a wise-guy wait staff, and a mixed-race jazz band that played offbeat versions of the music. It was so pleasingly unconventional that one young guy I talked with called it a new-generation hangout, a "beat" joint. I didn't exactly know what that meant, but I loved the place anyway.

A booth became free, and I quickly moved to occupy it. When I looked up, ready to light a new cigarette, I was face-to-face with Jeannie again.

"What are you waiting for, doll? Take a seat—you're only a half hour late."

"Sorry, but Pittman never lets me leave on time. He always finds something else for me to do."

"You need a stiff drink. What will you have?" My waiter stopped over.

"Bring me a vodka martini," she said. The waiter smiled. "Vodka instead of gin? At last, Matt, you bring in a guest with class and taste."

A smoke was the next item on her agenda. I lit hers and then

I lit mine.

"How could you work for a guy like Pittman? You seem like someone who's her own person and wouldn't tolerate some disagreeable, domineering asshole."

"You know the answer, Matt. It's called money: I have to make a living."

"Yeah, I know that story intimately. And I've seen the other side, too. Money can contaminate, corrupt, and kill. Just ask my clients."

"Do you make good money as a private eye? Do you like the work of serving clients?"

"I make enough to pay my bar tabs and keep the bill collectors happy. It's hard to answer your other question, though, because I'm not really sure. What I do enjoy is solving cases. It's a real accomplishment to complete the puzzle, fix the broken, find the missing part, clean up the mess—and always do it in my own way. Clients tend to get themselves—and other humans—into a lot of tough fixes. I guess it's my job to try and save them—sometimes from themselves."

"Is your work dangerous?"

"No, not most of the time. It's no more dangerous than a game of Russian Roulette." She didn't know how to react at first, but then she laughed uneasily.

"How about another drink?" She said yes, and I signaled the waiter for two more.

"Jeannie, may I get personal for a minute?"

"Sure, take longer if you like." She took an expectant drag on her cigarette.

"Bloodshot eyes look good on you."

"Oh, you monster," she said in an incongruously light voice. She also smiled at the beast.

"That was a compliment. I was trying to say that you look pretty even under tough circumstances—at the end of a long day."

"Thank you. How awkwardly but charmingly romantic."

"Thanks, doll—that's one of the nicest things anyone has ever said to me." Spouting gab like that, I could tell that I was approaching the edge of one too many drinks. Maybe another smoke would help straighten me out. "Okay, I'm done with that kind of stuff. Now, what was it that you wanted to talk to me about?"

"*Your* big baby blues?"

"No, no, let's save that for another time. I'm talking client business now."

"Oh, right." She acted as if she was dragging herself out of bed. "What I'm going to tell you is strictly between you and me. But if you do have to tell someone else, keep my name out of it."

"Of course. What do you take me for?"

"Julie Fischetti is alive and apparently well. She's working as a model...."

"Why the QT about that? Where is she working? Who is she modeling clothes for?"

"Ah, she works for us at Entertainment Services. But she doesn't model clothes."

The liquor had slowed my suspiciousness. "Then what does she model? You don't mean...?"

"She literally provides an entertainment service—Julie is one of our high-priced escorts."

Several ideas and questions assaulted my mind at once. I had to try and focus on one at a time. "Wait a minute: I know that some struggling actors and actresses freelance as prostitutes for extra money. But now you're telling me that Viogram, the corporation, runs its own, special hooker service? And that one of its supporting players is Julie Fischetti?"

Her words were crawling out now. She was reluctant to say them, and—at the same time—she wanted to give them the proper emphasis. "No, Matt, she's not a supporting player— she's a high-demand star. You see, the service offers a particular kind or flavor of sex: All the hookers are colored, and Julie seems to be the most popular one of them all."

"So Entertainment Services specializes in black sex for sale?"

"Well, I wouldn't say 'specialize.' It's just one of the many things the department does to boost corporate profits. It doesn't miss a trick. It reaches out to the public with movie souvenirs, board games, and film-adapted novels. But yes, it also uses the studio's most beautiful colored actors and actresses to sexually serve moneyed clients. It's a seven-night-a-week service: White Hollywood movers and shakers—male and female—come to get a private piece of forbidden fruit."

"But Julie signed a contract to make movies. What does this have to do with that?"

"I'm not a lawyer, but every contract makes vague references to related services that the signing player might have to undertake."

"Including sleeping on the job?

"Apparently." She killed the rest of her martini.

"What do customers shell out for this sex?"

"It depends on the partner they choose. I believe Julie's price runs at about $200 an hour."

I tried to whistle, but my mouth was dry. I needed another drink. I signaled the waiter to bring us refills. "And Julie is totally on board with this service?"

"Ah, I don't know her, Matt. I've seen her photos and heard reports about her, but I've never spoken to her."

"Where is she? How can I reach her?"

"I'm verbally exhausted. Can't we talk about that a little later?"

I felt that there was a lot left unsaid. And I couldn't get my mind to unthink about the many possibilities. But my little informer was upset—she needed some personal attention. "You sure know a lot, dearie. Knowledge is power."

"I don't have any power; I just know what I hear. My boss is the power. He even has the ear of Spencer Morgan. They talk all the time."

"That probably means the guy at the top knows all about this sex service. I guess I shouldn't be surprised. What do you think about it all?"

"Nothing. I've become cynical. It's everyday life—Hollywood style."

"Make that *corporate* Hollywood style. But the cynic in you surprises me. I pictured you as an idealist," I tried to joke.

She didn't get the joke. "Matt, I can't relax here. There are too many people. How about if we go to my place? I can offer you good company, plenty to drink, and even something to eat if you wish."

"I'm game—let's go. We'll take your car, and then I'll cab it back."

She lived in a light-gray apartment building not far from the little lake in increasingly fashionable Echo Park, about three or so miles east of downtown. Her apartment was conventionally laid out, with each room painted a different pastel color. There was no balcony, but the place was conveniently modern, solidly clean, and quiet. While it probably didn't cost what my place did, it surely came with a sizable price tag. In fact, the apartment, its new furniture, its vases of fresh flowers, all its clever feminine knick-knacks, and the 1949 Dodge in its parking lot outside strongly suggested that Miss Goodwin made a good living at Viogram Pictures. I mentally applauded her—that was an "A" plot development in my mind.

I sat down on her fluffy brown sofa and watched her take control of things.

"I don't have scotch, Matt. Is bourbon okay?"

"That's fine, but skip the water, though. What are you drinking now?

"The same as you, but I want mine on the rocks."

"Did you drink vodka martinis and bourbon on the rocks back in the Midwest?"

That stopped her cold. "How did you know I came from the Midwest?"

"Your flat accent. Your practical sensibility. Your newly acquired cynicism. But I didn't even need to recognize those or other obvious qualities. The Midwest seems to be where most transplanted Angelenos come from."

She brought me my drink and curled up in the matching fluffy chair across from me. She looked alluring in such a comfortable pose, and I knew she knew it. "I was born and raised in Ames, Iowa, but the place bored me out of my mind. It was too small, too narrow. I couldn't imagine living out my days there—it would have been like a surrender."

"Surrender? So you took your personal battle to LA, hoping to land an opportunity in the movies?"

"Oh, no! Becoming a movie star has never been an ambition of mine. While I knew I was attractive, I also realized early on that I didn't have the high-level looks a young woman needs to get noticed in Hollywood. And besides, I can't act worth a damn—it's impossible for me to fake anything, even being happy. I couldn't do it in Ames, and I can't do it here."

"Who cares what Hollywood wants or thinks? You're a star to me."

She tried to look inside me. "Thanks, Matt. Are all private eyes so sweet?"

"No, they're unfeeling and uncaring. It's just that I know how to act...." We both laughed.

"What role do I play in your story?'

"You're a central character—everything starts with you."

"Do I get to be romantic with the hero?"

"Oh, I never thought about that," I said with a straight face. "There—aren't I a great liar? That's acting, right?"

"You're funny, too. Where were you born, Mr. Moulton?"

"I'm a Midwesterner, just like you. I was born and raised in Chicago."

"That's a different kind of Midwest. The place is sophisticated. And it's bigger than LA and Ames put together."

"Yes, and it's a hard-assed town. But I didn't leave Chicago for LA directly. I moved to San Francisco after the war, got myself into dead serious trouble with the powers there, and escaped to the City of Angels last year. So now we find ourselves here together—two escapees with a little money but nowhere to go."

"There's still hope for us." She accidentally—on purpose— spilled some of her drink on her pink blouse. "I'm so clumsy!" She brushed at the wetness with her napkin. "Oh, excuse me while I go change my clothes."

My stomach was staging a minor rebellion, growling for some nourishment. I needed a real meal or a reasonable facsimile. But it was hard to break away from the momentum of the day—and now night. The alcohol in my empty stomach was going right to my head, a place that was supposed to be sober and on the job.

Keeping myself clearheaded and dispassionate became even harder when Jeannie returned to the living room. She was wearing a long, silky pink robe, but it was completely unbuttoned, revealing a sweetly developed, long-legged body covered only by a half-bra and very brief panties. She brought me another drink and tiptoed back to her chair, leaving behind that unmistakably earthy scent of sex. I was aroused by the smell, sight, and even sound of it all. I couldn't say a word.

While there was a lot of beautiful body to look at, I couldn't take my eyes off her feet. Their curvaceous, sultry-toed, high-step anatomy was so provocative that you really couldn't accurately call them bare feet—they were nothing if not naked, and that probably would have gotten them banned as obscene in some of the more sexually frigid and rigid states.

"You have beautiful feet, sweetheart."

She took a drink. "Oh, Matt, be serious. You're always joking."

How could I convince her I was serious? I walked over, bent down on my knees, took her right foot in my hand, and started stroking it. Then I kissed it, again and again, slowly and passionately. She apparently got the message and started moaning, as if her feet were the most sexually sensitive part of her body. With that encouragement, I put my lips around her red-polished toe. She loved that, too, and so I soon devoted the same kissing and sucking attention to her left foot.

My lovemaking was working its way up. I slipped off her panties and started kissing and caressing her lower lips—no surprise, they were way more sensitive to my touch than her

80

feet were. I advanced to her pointy breasts and removed that little bra—it was just in the way. Why women wore bras, I could never figure out. Ultimately, I came face-to-face with her as I did in the office early in the day, and I acted the way I wanted to then: I took her face in my hands and started kissing her mouth and sucking her lips. She returned the compliment, and—if anything—acted even more lustfully than I did.

We were past the lovemaking point of no return. The problem was that we weren't equally well dressed for the occasion. Jeannie was dressed for love—she had nothing on. I was dressed for a business interview: Wearing my shirt, tie, and suit pants, I was still a human resource, not a love partner. But Jeannie slowly, sensuously took care of that. She wouldn't allow me to remove my own clothes. She took them off piece by piece, devoting loving attention to each body part and space they covered. I hadn't felt so titillated in a long time. The irony was that I had partly expected that a sexual encounter with Jeannie was going to be mainly business, a way to elicit information. So much for that idea. Instead, I was a kid who opened the door to the classroom and discovered a candy land in its place.

We enjoyed a sweet two hours, but now we were full, still a little drunk, and very tired. She lay in my arms, her now bushy blonde head pressed to my chest. I was in an odd state of suspension, feeling paralyzed physically and rejuvenated mentally. All the action was now in my mind, and a lot was happening.

"Hey Matt dear, do you have to be so loud?" She whispered.

"Was I breathing too hard?"

"No, I could hear you thinking. Do you ever rest?"

I laughed at her aural insight. "I'm sorry—my brain is a

loudmouth. I've warned him about that before...."

"What were you thinking about?"

"The long day and the short night—and how to wed the two."

"What do you mean?"

"I guess I mean a lot of things. For example, I was thinking about what a risk you took to reveal that stuff about Julie and Viogram. Why did you do it?"

She was quiet for a long few seconds. "I wanted to be honest—telling you was the right thing to do." Then she looked up at me with that fetching but serious face of hers. "Besides, I like you—and I wanted you to succeed at your case."

"I see."

"Did I do okay?"

"Yes, of course, you were honest, and I appreciate that. As you said, you don't know how to lie. But sweetheart, you do know how to conceal, don't you?"

Her voice rose above the whisper: "What do you mean?"

"You didn't tell me the whole story, did you? That's what I'm waiting for tonight."

She buried her head more deeply into my chest and stayed silent there for about a minute. Then she sighed, sat up, and stretched across the bed to her cigarette case on the little end table. She took out a smoke, lit it, and took a long, hard drag. She looked ready to talk.

"I'm sorry, Matt. I meant to tell you everything, but I just didn't know how to go about it—how to say it." She tried to focus her thoughts as she picked off a piece of tobacco from her tongue. "It's like this: Julie is not working as an escort voluntarily. She's being blackmailed into doing it. So is the rest of the escort staff." She searched my face for a reaction.

I didn't surrender a look, but I was stupefied. What she

had told me before was unpleasant. And while I had strongly assumed there was more bad information to come, I didn't expect something as unsavory, as outrageous, as this. "What's Viogram holding over Julie's head? What's the blackmail?"

"I heard Pittman refer to the carrot and the stick. I honestly don't know what stick they're using on Julie. But the carrot is obvious: the prospect of future movie roles if she properly plays her part in the sex service."

"What about the others? Do you have any specific examples of Viogram using the stick on them?

Jeannie became as quiet as death. She was either pondering the question or fighting it—probably both. Being a snitch was hard, even when it was the right thing to do. She finally answered: "There's a young Negro actor named William Jones who used contract advances and company loans to feed his gambling habit. Finally, to pay off the growing debt, including interest, he had to agree to turn tricks as an escort for Entertainment Services."

"I'm guessing that they knew about his gambling obsession when they advanced and loaned him the money. They were setting him up for the blackmail."

"You're probably right, Matt," she said in a resigned manner.

"Where does this sex happen?"

"In a company mansion in Beverly Hills."

"And where does Julie live? How can I reach her?" I struggled to sit up, took one of Jeannie's smokes, and lit it.

She just looked at me and looked at me, with the seeming hope that I'd change my mind and say "forget about the questions for now."

"Well, she and all the other escorts live in the mansion, each more or less confined to his or her own bedroom."

I laughed wearily and shook my head. "This is just too much. Have you thought this out, sweetheart? Ninety years after the end of the Civil War, in the middle of liberal Hollywood, this movie studio—your employer—has revived black slavery. Sex slavery no less." I got up and started walking around the bedroom. "The studio even maintains its own plantation, keeping its slaves in a mansion in Beverly Hills. I'm surprised your boss doesn't rename himself Robert E. Lee. It would be poetic justice."

She held the cigarette close to her mouth, but she was too far away—mentally—to take a drag. "I knew the details of what was going on. But I didn't put everything together until I started telling you the Julie story earlier this evening. I guess I had been blind."

"No doll, you weren't blind. In a sense, you just kept the sunglasses on during the smog and into the night. They nicely darken and blur the stuff you don't want to know, don't want to see. I'd wear them, too, except then I'd never solve a single case. I'm already in the dark; I don't need to make things worse."

As we talked about all this, we sat facing each other on the bed naked to the world. I thought it was a great way to work, if a bit distracting. She seemed totally comfortable with it, too.

"What puzzles me is how Viogram has gotten away with this operation. I know the cops are highly selective in what they enforce and who they go after for bad behavior, but the revelation of something like this—a Negro sex slavery ring in the middle of Hollywood—would not be good news for the force. Politicians and the press would start openly wondering about the LA police and whether it thought it was working in 1850, rather than 1950. And they'd have a great point."

"So what do you plan to do now, Matt?"

"That's easy. I'm going to do my job, the work I've been paid to perform: Find Julie and bring her home. Nothing more, nothing less. Now, if people get in my way, then my approach changes. With what I know now, and what I may learn later, I'd be happy to open my mouth and cause trouble for people, everything from public embarrassment to legal difficulty. We'll see what's necessary."

"And what about us?"

"Well, I don't know how you feel, sweetheart, but I kind of like us right now. I think we have passion on our side. I'd like to keep seeing you—at least until we reach the point that we can't stand each other any longer."

She laughed. "If that's your way of asking for a date, Matt, my answer is yes."

I embraced her and kissed those eyes. "Please write down your phone number and the address of that sex house."

"You'll need the password to get into that place."

"What is it?"

"Mediterranean Night."

"It sounds like a stolen painting—a second-rate one." I started looking for my clothes, which were strewn over the floor. One sock was in the corner.

"Are you getting ready to go?"

"Yes, I'm starving. I have to find someplace to eat."

"Oh, Matt, I can make you something."

"No, I wouldn't be very good company for you. I'm caught up in a lot of high-level thinking right now—how best to put one foot in front of the other in this intensifying case. I'll grab a bite at that diner we passed around the corner. Is it still open?"

"It's an all-night place."

"Good, I'll feel right at home there."

Chapter Ten

Glendale Boulevard never goes to sleep. But it was now past Midnight on a weekday, and so the street was at least nodding off. The few cars on the road crawled along as if they were lost. The few pedestrians strolled and wandered, though a couple of people were quick in step, as if someone or something was following them. In the middle of all that relative peace emerged the two-storefront diner known as Eddie's Eats. The place assaulted passersby with a buzzing, highly electric light—it was so bright that it lit up half the block. Eddie's was as wide-eyed as a nervous insomniac.

I walked into the empty place and sat down at the long counter. Behind it, at the other end, the waiter/cook—perhaps it was Eddie—lingered over a newspaper. He acted as if I didn't exist. Finally, unprompted, he decided to fold the newspaper and reluctantly shuffle over in my direction. The guy was on the South end of fifty, with thinning, graying black hair and a face and body that were as flabby as bread dough. The word that best defined him, however, was oily: He had greasy hair and a greasy complexion. Too bad some of that oil didn't make it into his manner.

"Okay, waddya need, Bud?"

"What do I need? Well, you can start by bringing me a menu.

And if you're not too busy, you can give me a cup of coffee."

He rolled his eyes and reached behind the counter for a badly worn menu. He then flipped my cup and filled it with steaming hot coffee. It smelled burnt. But the worst thing was that Eddie wouldn't leave: He loomed over me as I reviewed the menu.

I just wanted to get rid of the guy, so I quickly tried to order something.

"What's the hot turkey sandwich like?"

"What can I say, it's turkey and it's hot." He didn't seem very tough—he was more hard-bored than anything else.

"Okay, give me the hot turkey."

"You don't want the fried potatoes, do you?"

"In fact, I do."

He rolled his eyes again, swiped the menu out of my hand, and shuffled off to the kitchen. His departure robbed him of the opportunity to patently ignore his next customer, a man in a dark suit who just walked in the door.

But this guy was hard to ignore. Like Rose Fischetti's Josh, he approached wall-to-wall and floor-to-ceiling in size. He differed from Josh only in being both lighter and darker: He was White and looked more openly intimidating. The man had only one expression, that of embittered ferociousness. And I couldn't stop staring at that bulge above his eyes. It was just a protruding forehead, one of Nature's terrible tricks, but it looked like some kind of weapon—and a deadly one at that. Despite all the ominousness, he simply sat down at the end of the counter, folded his hands, and waited for service.

A few minutes later, Eddie brought me my dinner. The turkey sandwich was open-faced and drenched in gravy, and so I couldn't just pick it up and eat it. This was a knife and fork job—but that required concentration, which I couldn't provide

87

right now. I was too busy paying attention to the other side of the counter, where the big guy was whispering something into Eddie's ear. He made those nothings sweet by offering Eddie what looked like a $20 bill. Mister Oily took it and then disappeared into his kitchen.

The big guy stood up and lumbered in my direction. He ignored me and went right to the jukebox and spent a minute there agonizing over all the choices. Finally, he selected Lena Horne singing "One for My Baby (and One More for the Road)." It was a great song, but it was playing too loud. I couldn't hear myself think, though that was not what it was meant to drown out. Suddenly, I was being poked in the back again, and this time it wasn't Jeannie.

"Hey Charlie, where do you come off sticking your nose in other people's business?" He bent himself in half to put his face right next to mine.

"You've got the wrong guy. I don't know you, and I don't know your people."

"Then why were you creeping around them today?"

"I don't know what you're talking about. Now shove off, pal, I'm busy."

That wasn't the right answer. The mass man grabbed my neck with one paw and the gun under my jacket with the other. He threw the gun across the room and put his now free paw around my neck. He then lifted me off the seat and began squeezing me as if he were trying to make dick juice. Whether by mistake or design, his hands clasped the bottom of my neck where he couldn't choke off my air as quickly as he could have done with his hands a little higher.

Whatever the truth, I wasn't going to surrender my last breath to him easily. The fingers of my left hand dug hard into his right eye. If I could get that lid up, I'd yank the eye right out of his head. With my energy fast depleting, I then plunged my right hand toward his crotch, and I got lucky: I found his member, and it was fully erect. The guy was apparently a pervert, getting a sexual kick out of torturing and perhaps killing me—and, worse, doing it to a Lena Horne love song. I got a good grip on his manhood and pulled on it like there was no tomorrow, like it was a jammed handle on the last cigarette machine. He shrieked and dropped me to the floor. The jerk-off was now doubled over, and so I violently delivered my knee into his face. It felt like I had struck iron and shattered my knee. But it sent Eddie's friend backwards, into my counter stool. I then walked over and kicked him in the face. That was for my neck burns.

I easily retrieved my gun, but I barely got my breath back—I'd never take oxygen for granted again.

Somehow, I managed to choke out some words. "Hey Eddie, get out here now!

He didn't dawdle this time. "What is it?"

"Get me your phone."

He pulled it out from behind the counter, and I dialed and waited.

"Hello, LA Detective Bureau."

"Is Lieutenant Pascal in the office?"

"Who's calling?"

"Tell him Matt Moulton."

It must have been a slow night because Pascal came to the phone in seconds. "What's up, Matt?"

"You wanted a lead in the Sykes case? I think I got you one: He's lying here on the floor of Eddie's Eats on Glendale Boulevard. He tried to torture me or rub me out with his monstrous size, but that didn't work."

"Is he still breathing?"

"Oh yeah. And I'm sure he's dying to answer all your questions, beginning with where he was last night."

"What's this all about? Why did he attack you?"

"I'm not sure. But you know I'm working for a client, and you know that's a confidential matter."

"If a crime has been committed...."

"Brad, I haven't violated any LA laws, and neither—to my knowledge—has the person who hired me. If any of that changes, you'll be the first one I'll call. Goodbye, lieutenant."

I put my gun on the counter, moved my plate to another stool place, and resumed eating. The turkey was still warm, and it was actually tasty. Eddie really knew how to cook, or at least how to reheat stuff. Everybody was good for something.

The next day, I spent hours mentally preparing for my evening performance at Viogram's black sex plantation. I would have to pretend to be a mover/shaker kind of guy willing to spend big money on "forbidden" fun. Then, once I found Julie, I would try to find a way to sneak her out of there. It was going to be a challenge, and Sara wouldn't let me forget it.

"If it killed Sykes and intended to kill you, Viogram is as ruthless as the Mob. It's just another form of organized crime," said Sara, before she blew on her coffee.

"Yeah, but how organized is that? Why do away with Sykes, one of its own actors? And trying to rub me out for just asking a few questions is pure Amateur Hour."

"Still Matt, Viogram plays rough. And it obviously knows who you are."

"But Pittman and his huge henchman won't be there. They're the only people who can identify me. And I'll be pretty well disguised tonight in a well-tailored black suit I used to wear when I went nightclubbing with Gina. It's not formally formal, but it does a great job of making me look like a man of means who's out on the evening. My name will be Michael Holland. Doesn't that sound rich? For this performance, I could win an Oscar."

"Or lose a life. Be very careful."

"I'll make a note of it." I was as worried as she was.

Chapter Eleven

There was no more desperate place in America than the obscenely wealthy city of Beverly Hills. It seemed to starve for attention. Its residents—most of whom were associated with Hollywood as big stars of some kind— weren't content with just living well—they were determined to live as large and as loud as life would allow. Their gaudy properties stretched for acres. They had private roads, private forests, multiple swimming pools, and elaborate European-style fountains. The home of one Beverly Hills client of mine had twenty bathrooms. She probably needed them to dispose of all the coffee she drank, the coffee she couldn't sugar herself (she had a special maid to do that). Yet, she and my other Beverly Hills clients were among the unhappiest people I had ever worked for. All the green and all the flash and all the pretension failed to pay off for them. That was why I felt FDR might have gotten it wrong. It wasn't our poor and unemployed who needed help—it was our rich and powerful. What could we do to help them feel better about themselves so that they didn't have to show off and act out all the time? That was what Beverly Hills was all about —the drama and the struggle of the poor, poor rich.

I stopped at the gate of my address on Bliss Canyon Road.

Two rough-looking uniformed guards carefully looked me over and demanded to know my business. I gave them the Mediterranean Night password, and that caused them to break out in smiles. "Go right in, you bad boy," their look seemed to say. I responded with my own look that said, "thank you for letting me in to case your joint."

After two curves of the private road, the Viogram mansion came into view. It was a sprawling, low-rise stone castle, complete with turrets or little towers. It sat behind a lawn that was the size of a public park, and it flowed into driveways that were wider than some city streets. A man was parking his car on a concrete lot just off the driveway, and I quickly parked behind him. Maybe I could avoid being singled out by strolling in with the guy. I didn't get out of my car until he left his, and then I followed him—through private birds standing, walking, hopping, and flying around everywhere—to the castle door. He rang the doorbell, turned around, and said "hello" to me. The guy seemed like a vintage Hollywood decision maker—short, round, and overdressed for the occasion. A premium unlit cigar protruded from his lips, suggesting that he might have been an executive producer—someone who never stopped playing his daytime role.

A stiff butler opened the door and let us in to an enormous, high-ceilinged foyer. After the movie-style manservant took our hats, a tall middle-aged guy in a tuxedo rushed in to greet my inadvertent companion. His grudging smile highlighted the gray hairs in his mustache.

"Mr. Smith, how are you?"

"Very fine, and yourself?"

"I'm doing well. How are things at MGM?"

"They're going grand. We have some big hits coming up."

"Good, good. How are the wife and kids?"

"They went to the movies tonight to see "Cinderella"—for the third time. They can't get enough of that Walt Disney stuff."

"Of course, of course. Well, go right in, Mr. Smith."

The host then approached me. "I don't believe we've ever met. My name is Ralph Norton, I'm here to help satisfy your needs this evening."

"How kind. I'm pleased to meet you." I shook his extended hand. "My name is Michael Holland."

His little black eyes gave me a doubtful, searching look—this guy was either especially suspicious of me or simply skeptical about anyone new. I didn't know anything about being a high-priced pimp, but I guessed that it wasn't good business to give potential customers the visual third degree.

"What do you do, Mr. Holland?"

Now it was time for the con. "You could call me an independent producer. I help finance pictures, particularly race films."

"Oh, race films. Which ones have you done?" This guy wouldn't stop.

"I've done a number of small ones. But the biggest one I helped finance was *Stormy Weather* for 20th Century Fox." If Fox hadn't used outside financing for that film, and he knew it, I was in trouble.

"Oh yes, 'Stormy Weather,' it's one of my favorite musicals." He dismissed his doubt for now. "Please come in."

He directed me into a parlor, a large, jasmine-smelling room that was considerably more modern and intimate than the foyer promised it might be. It was decorated and furnished in the whites, blacks, and silvers of the Art Deco style that was so popular before the war. There was a large silver swirl bar in the corner, manned by a guy mixing the MGM man's drink, and a large silver chandelier over the center of the room. What was most striking about the room, however, was how labor-intensive it was. To serve two customers, Viogram needed four workers, and that didn't even include the escorts and others to come. The four included two very young, impeccably dressed thugs. They were there to keep things dishonest, and the guns packed under their jackets helped guarantee that.

"Mr. Holland, what are you drinking tonight?" asked Norton.

"I'll go with scotch and soda."

He relayed my order to the barman. This was either person-alized service or overkill—maybe he also helped customers take their clothes off.

A few minutes later, a fifth worker—a more domesticated-looking heavy—brought the enslaved entertainment into the room: Eight black escorts, five women, and three men. Not a single one was anywhere near thirty years old, and they were all beautiful or handsome in ways that probably drew a lot of second looks everywhere they went. They stood next to each other in the center of the room, with Julie on the far end from me. I almost didn't recognize her because she looked taller and leggier than her pictures suggested she'd be. Her fluffy but form-enhancing black dress helped create that longish effect and made her seem more endlessly sexy than the other women on display. She also looked more human than the Julie in the publicity photos—the one in the flesh looked a little drained and very vulnerable.

Norton turned to Mr. MGM first. "Who would you like to socialize with this evening, Mr. Smith?"

Smith made up his mind quickly: He put his hands on the

chest of a brawny man with light eyes, who looked like a young, black version of Clark Gable. "I'll take Charlie, of course," he said, as he stroked that chest. Charlie didn't seem overjoyed.

"Charlie? Oh yes, he's your very favorite," said Norton. "Anything to drink tonight?"

"Bring me a bottle of your finest champagne and two glasses." He gave special emphasis to the word "two" as if that made him a combination of Jesus Christ and Santa Claus.

"And Mr. Holland, who will be your companion?"

I pointed to Julie. "I choose this young lady."

"Great choice. Her name is Julie. Julie, this is Michael Holland."

"I'm all yours, Michael," she said in a provocative tone. Julie really could act.

"Anything more to drink, Mr. Holland?"

"I'll take another scotch and soda. And you, Julie?"

"A glass of red wine."

Drinks in hand, Julie led me on a long walk up a winding staircase, through another parlor and a kind of sitting room, down a long, wide hall, and finally into her bedroom. It was the size of a small apartment, but—based on what I spotted in the closet and the drawers—it had to serve as her whole world. It was her home, her workplace, her prison cell. The room looked expensive in a cherry red kind of way, but it lacked an individual person's personality. It was designed to comfort the customers, and so everything gravitated toward the huge bed, which could probably have accommodated four large people with room to spare. I was trying to figure out what kind of sex required so much space when Julie distracted my attention.

She started to kiss my neck as she slipped off my jacket. "Tell me what I can do for you."

"Well, you can begin by not rushing things. Why don't you just take a seat, precious?"

"But we only have an hour, unless you want them to bill you for more."

"An hour is plenty of time for what I have to do."

She sat down reluctantly, with a confused look in her watery eyes. "I can't place you. Are you from behind the scenes? Or have you been in actual movies? You look familiar...."

I laughed. "No, I'm not Hollywood sweetheart. But I appreciate the affectionate enthusiasm you just showed me."

She still looked at me as if I was some kind of star, though that didn't seem to be a big deal to her. I suspected that she had already served more than her share of them.

"We have more important things to talk about: Are you allowed to leave this place at the end of each day?"

"What? Why is that your business? WHO are you?" After the last word, she continued moving her mouth, as if she was hungry or thirsty for something.

"Please answer my question, Julie."

"I live here; I have nowhere else to go." She was still in a state of chewing.

"Do you like this work? Is this what you want to do with your life?"

She got up and started walking around. She tried to light a cigarette but then decided against it. "If you must know, I do this work to get ahead. It will lead to parts in movies. Maybe even big parts."

"Is that what Viogram tells you?" I smiled and then fired up my own smoke.

"Yes, and why would they lie to me? I've already been in two of their movies." She continued her hyperactive movements, sitting down and then quickly getting up again.

"What does sexually serving clients have to do with acting in the movies? I don't see the connection, sweetheart."

She raised her voice for the first time. "Why are you asking me these questions? Are we ever going to fuck?" She practically shouted out that last question.

"I want to know more about you."

She sat down and grew quiet again, withdrawing within herself. "Who are you?"

"I'm a private dick—your mother hired me to find you and bring you back home. She's been frantic over your disappearance."

Her dark skin seemed to pale. "Oh, Mom, of course. I should have expected she'd come look for me." She was also getting a little shaky, which could have been a natural reaction to emotional news about family. But I suspected that the emerging shiver might have another cause.

"You have to understand something, Mr. Holland, or Michael. My mother doesn't want to see me become a star." She started to slur a little bit, though she had yet to take one sip of her wine. "In fact, she doesn't want to see me do anything on my own. Mom plans to control me, like she controls everybody else. She's the hood in hose...."

I killed my drink. "I won't get involved in the psychological politics of family relations. I see them in cases all the time, but they're business for a mind doctor, not a dick. I was hired to concern myself with your disappearance, which your mother has every right to worry about."

She dropped her drink and acted as if she was going to cry about it. "Oh, no, oh goodness." She bent over and looked at the broken glass and spilled wine, but then stood up, stepped away, and looked for her pack of cigarettes.

"Would you like one of mine?"

"No, thanks, I have my own." She put a cigarette in her mouth and lit it with an unsteady hand.

"Now that I've found you, I've discovered another problem—your studio has turned you into a slave. Have you admitted that to yourself? That Viogram has essentially put you in chains to sexually serve whoever demands it? You criticized your mother for being a criminal, but what about your bosses—what are they?"

Her mouth still seemed in a state of longing. "Yes, but my current position here is just temporary. I'll be acting soon. All it takes is one good role, and then I'm on my way to a fabulous career."

"Well, I can't let you remain a 'temporary' slave. It's my job to get you out of here as soon as I possibly can."

"What happens if I don't want to go?" She said, with her voice raised again.

"Julie, your mind is scrambled: You don't seem to realize the distress you're in right now. And you apparently don't know what's happened already. Have you heard about Michael?"

She looked directly at me for the first time in a while. "What about him?"

"He was beaten to death a couple of nights ago."

"No, no!" She closed her eyes and put the knuckles of her fist in her mouth.

"I'm not the police, but I strongly believe that Viogram had him bumped off. Add murder to their rap sheet."

In seconds, she went from grieving to defiant again. "Well, I told him to stop fighting me about Viogram. He wanted me to abandon my contract and return to Chicago. He kept calling the studio. Threatening the people there. Promising he'd report them to the police. He was trying to control me as much as Mom had. Everybody wants to control me, even you."

"So the fact that you didn't want to be controlled and Viogram didn't want to be threatened—that justifies his murder?"

"I didn't say that!" Her face became very wet, as sweat beads emerged and teardrops fell.

"Was Michael ever part of this escort ring here?

She used her hand to wipe her eyes and then fan her face. "No, he refused to participate, even if it meant movie parts later on."

Her erratic thinking and behavior during our short time together worried me. I felt as if I was witnessing a breakdown, both mental and physical. Then the possible awful truth occurred to me. I grabbed her left arm. She swatted me with her right. However, I gripped tighter and pushed up her dress sleeve to confirm my suspicion: She had needle track marks.

"What drug are you injecting? Heroin?" She twisted her arm out of my grip with a flourish.

"Yeah, so what about it? It makes me relax and feel good. The world seems like a much better place—it becomes much easier to accept."

"Until you need another fix and can't get it right away. Then you start falling apart like you've done here tonight." She dragged on her cigarette and started pacing around again.

"Who got you started on this? Someone from Viogram?"

She rolled her eyes and laughed. "Do you ever stop questioning people? Let me be honest with you, Michael: You're a lousy date. Did any woman ever tell you that?"

"This is no joke, dearie. Think of how far you've come. In

100

pursuit of movie fame, you've reduced yourself to being a slave and a dope addict. It looks as if you're further away from your goal than ever."

Reality finally smacked her in the face—and it hurt. She lowered her head, put a hand to her eyes, and started sobbing.

"And you have to recognize who the real enemy is. It's not me—it's Viogram. I suspect that they got you started on your addiction. And I know they've paid big and worked hard to keep you there. It's all for one reason—so that they can continue selling your black body to an elite crowd in Hollywood."

She was still struggling to fight the truth. "You put everything in such a negative light."

"I guess I do. On the other hand, I don't have to dwell on slavery and dope addiction too much. They both have PR problems—and for good reason. They're Hell without the dying, although that can easily happen, too. But you really know all that already, don't you?"

She looked down and said, "And what's my alternative to all this? I can't win no matter what."

"I'm going to take you back to Chicago. Once you're there, I encourage you to take a cure and then do whatever you want to do. In the end, you might decide to chuck your mom and her lifestyle and return to Hollywood for your movie dream. That's fine. But you'll be starting over again without slavery and drugs."

"If Viogram is such a terrible and determined enemy, how do you propose to get me out of here?" She wasn't too unstable and unfocused to see that that, indeed, was the rub.

"Unfortunately, I can't do it right now—there's too much muscle around. I'll find another time and another way. But

I had to see you today and let you know what's going on. Is there a way I can contact you?"

"No." Her words came out in jitters. "Ever since Michael kept calling here, they've stopped me from using the phone."

"You're a mess. Are they going to give you something to tide you over for the rest of the evening?"

"Yes, they will. And I can't wait."

I stood there and looked at her for a long minute. "Well, goodnight, Julie—I'll be back." I grabbed her shoulders and lowered my head to kiss her. I couldn't help it. I was a human and a man to top it. Even in her disintegrating state, she looked beautiful and desirable. I could see why she was the star of this forced sex show. But I wasn't going to exploit her any further by sleeping with her. I held her hand and left.

I closed the door and saw another thug—the fourth of the night, if you don't count Norton—approaching me from down the hall.

"If you're finished, I'll take you down to see Mr. Norton."

"Well, lead the way."

As we walked downstairs, I fantasized about putting my gun handle into his head. But that would have been stupid, and besides, I didn't even bring my .38 for fear of the telltale bulge it would have created in my jacket.

The thug knocked on a door, and we entered a book-lined room that they probably called the library. It made the place look respectable, and it was a joke. I could imagine the characters here knitting sweaters before I'd ever see them reading any books.

Norton sat behind a desk at the end of the room. He stood up to greet me with his odd smile, which lacked any warmth or even amusement. It was totally broke, a smile that should have filed for bankruptcy.

"Did you enjoy Julie, Mr. Holland?"

"Yeah, she's quite a skirt."

"Please have a seat."

"No, that's okay, Norton. Just tell me what I owe," I said in an arrogant tone.

He frowned, and that expression was rich. I didn't like him either. He handed me a receipt.

"Hmm, $250? So that means $50 for three drinks? I'll tell you, Norton, inflation's out of control. It's going to be the death of us yet. Well, I guess it's that or something else." I threw two hundreds and a fifty on his desk. "Good night." I strolled out and could feel his cold stare following me.

Chapter Twelve

Whenever I leaned toward seeking police help, I always took a pill and tried to talk myself out of it. I reminded myself that they'd ask me a lot of questions and that could and probably would compromise the confidentiality of my clients and contacts. And if the police really did help me, they'd act as if I owed my life to them, and they'd be forever coming back to me for information. I'd become an unpaid advisor and stoolie. But I couldn't talk my way out of police help in the Viogram case. I didn't have the muscle to get Julie out of her plight by myself. The police had the muscle for the job—and the law to back it up. And so I rushed to a pay phone to see if Pascal was awake on his usual 24-hour shift. He was, and I headed downtown.

Two slovenly detectives walked out of Pascal's office, and then I walked in. My favorite (or at least most tolerable) LA police officer was sitting behind his desk, not just smoking his cigarette but wearing it out—he dragged on it with malice afterthought.

"Hello Matt, how's life on the gumshoe beat? Have a seat."

I lit up my own burn. "Did you ever break the news to Sykes' dad?"

"Yes, of course. He took it very, very hard. I hate making

those calls." He killed the thought with a puff.

"Whatever happened with that monster man I turned over to you?"

"Oh yeah—Charles Kozlowski. He gave us only a vague alibi for the evening of Sykes' murder. He said nothing more. We're still working on him, but it's tougher than usual because he has a high-priced attorney who really knows his stuff."

"Have you drawn a bead on who may have hired him?"

"Not yet—but I'd love to know that." He leaned forward and looked into my eyes as if they were going to reveal something.

I looked away. "Brad, possibly related to that, how tough are you on prostitution?"

"Prostitution?" He laughed and acted as if that was beside the point. "Well, we largely ignore individual practitioners, but we crack down on the larger organized stuff."

"Good. I saw evidence of the larger stuff—a high-priced escort ring run by a studio."

He put his old cigarette out in its final resting place, just outside the ashtray. Then he lit a new one. "A movie studio?"

"That's right. And you'll want to know the aggravating factor: It's forced prostitution, and all the escorts are black."

His raised eyebrows and half smile suggested that he felt sorry for me. "Oh no Matt, not that Negro stuff again. What's wrong with you lately?"

"What do you mean 'Negro stuff?' 'Negro stuff?' I'm just telling you what I've found, giving you a valuable tip. I'm not making things up to score political points, or complicate your day. Why are you so dismissive? Aren't LA laws supposed to protect blacks, too?"

"Of course, we protect blacks, too." He seemed to wonder about that for a while, and then—with a little guilt and a lot of guile—he said, "What studio are you talking about and where do they run this supposed forced-sex ring?"

"It's Viogram, and they operate the business in Beverly Hills. I've been there and seen how it works."

"Beverly Hills? You know, we have no jurisdiction there."

"Brad, if you're going to do nothing, just come out and say it. But don't treat me like an idiot. You know that Viogram is based in LA. If you had evidence they committed a serious crime, you could pursue them to their sex den in Beverly Hills. And, if necessary, to cover yourself politically, you could formally seek the cooperation of the Beverly Hills Police. It happens all the time."

He returned to sucking on his cigarette—it gave him time to think. "Look, Matt, you know that we live in a company town—Hollywood makes everything happen here. Without it, this city would be nothing. So we're pressured—from the top—to give the industry a lot of room, cut it a lot of slack. I can't go busting in on a studio unless I have solid, irrefutable evidence of a crime."

"Oh, I see, there are two different laws here: One for Hollywood and one for everyone else. Won't that make organized crime angry? I know you'd raid them for prostitution in a minute, on the flimsiest of evidence."

"You're making me mad now, Matt. I don't make the rules; I execute them. And you weren't born yesterday. You know the way it works: The powerful and the privileged get a pass sometimes." He raised his voice: "I'm talking about the same kind of people that often hire you for jobs."

"Unlike you, I'm not paid to enforce the law, but I get your drift, Lieutenant. My question is this: Are there any limits to this pass that you give to the powerful? How about murder and attempted murder? Those crimes may have been committed to protect this prostitution business. I suspect that Viogram hired your Kozlowski to torture and kill Sykes, a studio contract player who didn't want to play ball as an escort."

"Do you have any real evidence connecting Kozlowski to Viogram?"

"No, I'm not the police, Brad. I don't have a large staff of detectives to investigate things like that."

"You're full of piss and vinegar tonight, aren't you Moulton? Okay, we'll look at the Viogram angle on the murder." He got up and started walking around, puffing on his cigarette along the way. "But tell me something, Matt, is your client one of the forced prostitutes at Viogram?"

"You mean one of the sex slaves? Yes, she's related to my client."

"What's her name?"

"Why should I tell you that if you aren't going to help me?"

"Well, did Viogram kidnap her off the street and force her into prostitution?"

"No, she worked for the studio as a contract player."

"Oh, a contract player. Might she have initially volunteered for the escort work as a way to get ahead in the movies?"

I couldn't answer that question, but I also couldn't let him score rhetorical points on me. "All I know is that she can't get away now, in large part because they're forcing drugs on her."

"Uh, huh." He sat back down and lowered his eyes. "The situation already seems vaguer and more ambiguous than you initially described it."

I found myself squinting through the fog of all that cigarette smoke. "Yeah, I guess you could talk yourself into seeing it that way. It helps you rationalize why you're not going to do something about corporate sex slavery."

He looked as if he was going to paste me with some blistering remark, but he apparently pulled it back and relaxed. Despite the hard time I always gave him, he probably liked me more than he could ever like anyone in what he saw as a partly shady, trouble-seeking, trouble-making business. "Why don't you go to the Beverly Hills Police with your story? After all, according to you, this sex ring is going on right in their own back yard."

"I don't know what I'm going to do, Brad. Beverly Hills Police will tell me the same thing you did—and you weren't entirely wrong. Hollywood is in control here. They hold the keys to the prison. If it's possible, I'll have to find a way to pick the lock."

He smiled. "As long as you can keep it more or less legal, Matt."

"Oh, right. I almost forgot about the two different laws." I stood up with a defeated air.

"We'll have to go out for a drink next time."

"Sure thing. Later, lieutenant," I said as I dragged off into the night.

The next day still seemed like night—with the streetlights out. I didn't see a clear path forward, at least not yet. So I went into the office hoping to find inspiration there. It was the noon hour, and Sara was out, apparently grabbing a sandwich. It was a very hot day for October, and so I opened my inner office window, took off my jacket and gun holster, and hung them up on the coat rack. With a fresh drink in my hand, I could now sit down and comfortably dwell on my indecisiveness. The outer office door opened, but I couldn't see who entered because my door was halfway closed. I assumed it was Sara, and I was wrong.

The first thing I saw was a gun. The guy at the end of it was a mid-sized, middle-aged heavy with homely looks, aggravated by a bad shave and a poorly fitting hat. He was the Everyman gangster.

"Matt Moulton—we need to talk," he said, in a voice loud enough to be heard in Pasadena.

"Who are you?"

"That's not important. I'm just here to tell you that someone dislikes you so much that they don't want you around anymore."

"And they sent you to deliver the message—a guy who's probably a coward without a gun in his hand. How impressive."

He moved closer and tried to kill me with an ugly expression. "Where do you come off insulting me? If you're not careful, I'll plug you sooner rather than later. And that might make it a messy job. I don't like messy jobs." He continued delivering his patter at the top of his voice.

"Put your gun down and we'll settle this once and for all."

He laughed uncomfortably. "Why would I put this gun down? I'm going to kill you with it."

"Well, at least hand it over and I'll show you how to use it."

"I can see why you're not very popular, Moulton."

I saw his coming fate, but I had to be careful not to give it away with my eyes.

He learned the truth as soon as he felt the metal in his back. His face dropped, and his eyes looked pained.

"Don't move, you bastard. If you do, I'll blow you away," said Sara, with the gun in her hand. "Now, very carefully, toss your pistol across the room." He quickly did as he was told.

I didn't take kindly to people who pointed a gun at me in my office, and so I sprang up and double slapped him across the face. I then threw a fist into his belly and followed with another fist to his face. As he lay in pain and sorrow on the office floor, I politely asked him if he still planned to kill me with a gun. He said "no," but I retrieved his gun in case he changed his mind.

We'd need to call Pascal to come pick up the garbage, but I had to put first things first: I walked over and hugged Sara.

"Sweetheart, thanks for keeping me around for a while longer! But where in the world did you get this .32?"

"I was going to surprise you with it. I bought it a couple of days ago as something I'd keep in my desk just in case—you know, for security. I guess I assumed that I'd never have to really use it. But then this happened, and the situation scared me: I worried that if I made the wrong move, big mouth would panic and kill you. I had to be quiet, careful, and firm, and of course I had to be lucky, too," she said, in a flushed manner I had never seen in Sara before. The threat of death tends to take your breath away.

"He could have killed you, too, dearie. That's why what you did was so brave—I'm proud of you."

I addressed myself to the guy on the floor. "Hey, pal, are you listening to this? We're talking about true bravery here. You were beaten by the very best, a tough mother of two." Sara laughed and began to relax.

I picked up the phone to call the police, but then I thought I'd try Pascal first. I was surprised to learn that he was in the office and free to talk to me.

"Yeah, Matt: What is it now?"

"Why are you in the office so early?"

"I don't know—why are you working so late? Haven't you been to bed yet?"

I laughed. "We're both working all the time. I'm calling now

corporations. Their power was vast and anonymous—you couldn't trace it to specific people like you could with private ownership. And despite what some stockholders and other business types claimed, you never really knew what these companies were doing or why. Viogram was a relatively small corporation. But if it could secretly enslave and murder, what could much larger and more nimble corporations do? What was going on at Standard Oil, Ford, and other big concerns? Through the Fischetti case, I woke up to the nightmare of bad guys organizing and hiding behind the legal wall of corporate power.

At first, Spencer Morgan didn't appear to be one of those bad guys. He looked like a conservative businessman from Wall Street who had taken a 3,000-mile wrong turn on Sunset Boulevard. He was a tall, grayish blonde with a long neck, a broad face, and light green eyes that softened his serious demeanor. He was polite, well-dressed, and impeccably groomed. And he seemed clueless.

His real self emerged only gradually—after a minute or two. He acted too arrogant, too self-controlled, and too egocentric by half. Despite being out of place in Hollywood, the guy thought he knew everything and could best everyone. If he was well-bred and well-educated, the efforts went seriously wrong somewhere.

"Would you like a drink, Mr. Moulton? asked Morgan, as he strolled to the private bar in his office, which took up only half the second floor of the studio's corporate building. It was probably larger than any indoor set on the studio lot. There were paintings on the walls, expensive throw rugs on the floors, showroom furniture everywhere, and air conditioning that chilled the air even more effectively than Morgan himself. It was like the office of a rich private businessman, except the type of business wasn't clear. Viogram was in the movies, but Morgan's office apparently didn't want to advertise that fact.

"Yes, thanks. I'll take a scotch on the rocks."

"I stock the finest scotch available. It's Glenfiddich single malt—I seldom drink any other. Since it's the perfect drink for this time of the day, I think I'll have one, too."

He brought me a glass and then sat down behind his desk. I took a sip.

"Well, what do you think, Mr. Moulton?"

"Yes, it's scotch…." The room went silent. He expected me to extol the stuff.

"Well, it's the best…. Now, what can I do for you? Why would a private investigator be coming to see me?"

"Mr. Morgan, I like to speak directly and avoid any cute posturing. You know why I'm here. If you didn't know, you surely asked Pittman."

Morgan took a sip of his scotch. "It's something about a contract actress here at Viogram? I don't usually get involved in those kinds of personal details."

"How about when one of your Negro contract players disappears? And a dick traces her whereabouts to a Viogram mansion in Beverly Hills that's operating as a black escort service? And the contract actress is fed drugs to make sure she doesn't leave that sex job? And she's not alone—none of the other players can go anywhere either? Do you get involved in that kind of personal detail?"

He chuckled but didn't laugh, as if to politely tell me that my big joke was a bad one. "Oh, come now, Mr. Moulton, that sounds preposterous."

I finished my scotch. "You may not like the way it sounds,

but I've seen the way it looks. I was there and saw the captive escorts, including my drugged missing person. If you say you don't know about all this, you're either lying or you're a very bad manager. That slavery ring is one of your entertainment services. Ask Pittman again."

"Would you like another drink, Mr. Moulton?" I did, but I started to fear being secretly drugged. "No, thank you, Mr. Morgan."

Morgan took a cigarette out of his gold case and fired it up with his gold lighter. Then, perhaps unconsciously, he looked with a barely discernible smile at a framed photo on his desk and moved it without changing its position. I didn't know who the young woman in the photo was, but I suspected it to be Chairman Ruth Gettling Baines—in her salad days. "Yes, Mr. Moulton, we do provide entertainment to wealthier customers at our Beverly Hills location. They get the opportunity to spend time with some of our actors and actresses. But there's no prostitution there, forced or otherwise. I wouldn't permit such a thing in our company," he said, half-smiling with indifference.

I laughed because his spiel was truly funny. "Again, Morgan, I've already been to your place in Beverly Hills. After my hour of "entertainment," your pimp—Ralph Norton—billed me $250, and that's not a price you pay for sweet-talking and hand-holding. My date, the missing young woman, lived in the room in which she entertained, and she essentially wasn't allowed to leave it or speak with anyone outside the plantation." I lit a smoke, finding a way to do it with an old-fashioned ordinary match. "Now, personally, I don't know how you live with yourself overseeing a sex slavery operation—a black one, no less. But I'm not here to scold or preach or debate with you about the facts. My job is to free my client—now."

He opened his desk drawer, pulled out a file, slipped on a pair of black-rimmed glasses, and started reading. "Hmmm, so you client's name is Julie Fischetti?"

"That's right. Isn't that what the file says?"

"Yes, it appears that she's still legally committed to her Viogram contract." He acted as if he was just finding all that out right now. "I see we've advanced her a lot of money over the years. Of course, she'd need to pay all that back in money or services." He pretended to look through more of the file, but then he finally closed it and removed his glasses with a feigned thoughtfulness. "Well, I'll tell you what I'll do for you, Mr. Moulton. I'll release Miss Fischetti from her contract for a settlement amount." He gave me a benevolent smile.

"And what would this settlement amount be?"

"I'll release her from her contract for $25,000. That will make everything free and clear."

I laughed while blowing smoke in his face. "$25,000? There's no way she owes you that much money." I raised my voice: "What you want is a ransom payment."

He pursed his lips and shook his head. "Mr. Moulton, you have quite the imagination. Slavery. Prostitution. Ransom. Is there anything else you want to bring into your story?"

"Yes, let's try murder on for size. In fact, you guys tried to murder me twice and obviously fumbled it each time. You also apparently murdered Michael Sykes, one of your colored contract players. He talked too much."

There was no smile this time. Instead, he appeared surprised that I knew Viogram was behind the murder and attempted hits.

"Now you demand $25,000. How is my client supposed to come up with that kind of cash?"

"Well, isn't Julie's mother Rose Fischetti, the gangland boss from Chicago? I'm sure she has the money to buy out the contract."

"I'm sure she does, but I'd advise her not to pay it. Maybe we'd make out better by exposing Viogram's sex slavery to the public."

Now his face became animated—every feature seemed to move. "Publicity, Mr. Moulton? Yes, that would hurt us. But it would hurt Rose Fischetti just as much, maybe more. I don't think she'd want any more public attention than she already receives on a regular basis now." He probably spoke the truth for a change.

"Okay, Morgan, but let's put it this way: You're just hoping, hoping that she chooses to pay rather than tell. But don't necessarily count on it. You never know what people will do, especially worried and angered mothers. I'll inform her of your demands, and then we'll see what she does."

He stared away into the distance and almost seemed a little unnerved for a moment.

"I suppose you want this to be a cash settlement."

He didn't respond the right way. "Yes, it has to be cash, but you can't bring it here or to Beverly Hills," he said in a faraway voice.

"If it's a legitimate settlement, why are we doing it in secret?"

His self-assurance was back: He just looked at me coldly.

"That's a telling answer, Morgan. Anyway, if you want the money, we'll have to make the transfer when, where, and how I say it should be done. I don't intend to leave myself vulnerable to another murder attempt. And it wouldn't even be smart on your part: I've documented everything, and it would all be released upon my demise."

"When, where, how, why?" He was waving his right hand around and talking above his usual monotone. "I told you, Mr. Moulton, I don't get involved in the personal details. As Viogram's leader—it's one true leader—I plan and manage the company's success, nothing more. To get Julie Fischetti released...from her contract, you'll have to work out the ah, grimy details with my underlings, specifically, in this case, Charles Pittman. I'll let him know that I'm doing this favor for you."

I didn't know what he meant by "one true leader," and I sure wanted to find out. But for the moment, I had had enough of the meeting, and so I stood up to leave. "Well, thanks for the favor, Morgan." I italicized my voice on the word 'favor.' "Maybe I can do one for you sometime soon. Meanwhile, tell Pittman to expect my call. Good day." He looked a little smug, as if he had just dismissed a smartass subordinate who dared challenge him.

I knew that now was the time to have a talk with Albert J. Greenstein, Rose Fischetti's lawyer. I left a message for him at the Beverly Hills Hotel, and he called me back to arrange a meeting that evening in the bar of the hotel's legendary Polo Lounge, one of the places where Hollywood types go to watch each other eat, drink, and be merry.

The Beverly Hills Hotel on Sunset Boulevard was one of Hollywood's Technicolor productions. It was rich (of course), star-struck (of course), and literally full of vivid color. The place was decorated throughout in pink and green, with a light brown trim that slightly cut down on all the glare. It was a spectacle to be sure, but it certainly wasn't for everybody. If you were a dick whose mood tended toward the black and white, the Beverly Hills Hotel was a challenging place to be.

Greenstein said he'd meet me outside the Polo Lounge, but people were passing back and forth everywhere, and I didn't know how he expected to recognize me. Then, a tall, well-dressed, fat man with close-together eyes and a few wisps of gray hair hurried over to me. He was shaped like a child's toy top: He bulged in the middle but greatly thinned out at his small, narrow head and at his tiny dancer's feet. He had a determined look that suggested he was going to take *me* for a spin.

"Are you Matt Moulton?"

"Yes."

He extended his hand. "Hello, I'm Albert Greenstein. Let's go right in."

To get to the bar, we had to walk through the restaurant. Everybody there seemed to give us the once-over to see if we were somebody important. As we staked out a couple of bar stools, I actually thought I saw Gregory Peck. But I had my doubts because I knew that for every real star that lived in Hollywood, there were probably dozens of counterfeit ones. These were the people who played up a vague resemblance to an actor or actress to saunter around in strategic places seeking recognition from star seekers and autograph hounds. It was one of the trashier parts of the Hollywood game, a cheap and easy way to become a celebrity—or seem like one, anyway. But that meant that the Gene Tierney you stopped on Santa Monica Boulevard the other night might have actually been Abigail Ponkadillo from Lushton, Nebraska.

Once we ordered our whiskies and lighted our smokes, I immediately revealed to Greenstein what was on my mind.

"So you're the guy who put the big snoop on me."

He gave me a dazed look and a suppressed smile, as if he

couldn't quite figure out what I meant. When it finally hit home, he laughed in a rat-a-tat way. "Oh yes, Mr. Moulton, I looked you over backwards and forwards. I wanted to find someone who had successfully overcome a lot of danger and difficulty—like you did with your San Francisco experience, for example. I also needed someone who was, how shall I say it, cosmopolitan, someone who could work with different kinds of people in different kinds of places. You seemed to be the man I was looking for."

"Cosmopolitan? Is that what you call it? I guess I'm guilty as charged, Mr. Counsel."

Greenstein did everything with authority. He talked with it, drank with it, laughed with it, even signaled the bartender with it. "Ha, ha! Clever remark, Mr. Moulton. Now what else do you have for me?"

I proceeded to tell him the whole story about sex slavery and murder and Viogram's role in all of it. I described Julie's drugged-out mental condition and how much money it was going to cost to free her from her captors. Greenstein's reaction disappointed me, however. He didn't widen his eyes, shake his head, or let out a sigh. The guy didn't seem to be surprised by anything I told him. I wondered what happened to my storytelling ability. Then I asked myself, "Well, why would he be surprised by anything?" He was a mob lawyer. If I thought I had seen a lot, he'd match that and raise me everything. This was everyday life in his neck of the woods.

"Unless they demanded otherwise, we'd probably give them the ransom in fifty or hundred-dollar bills. If we went any smaller than that, the package would become too bulky." He was already assuming that Rose would automatically decide to pay the ransom. Well, night followed day, wasn't that right?

"That should be fine. The boss man essentially agreed that the money transfer would be on my terms. So now my terms will include hundred-dollar bills, the easier load. I'm also going to insist on a daytime handoff in a crowded setting. I'm not ready to lose my life, particularly to a studio that makes such rotten movies."

Greenstein didn't laugh or even smile. He just became more serious, putting his hand on my arm and looking me straight in the eyes as he said, "Even under such favorable conditions, make sure you bring a gun. The craziest things can always happen."

"Oh yes, I'll be armed. I prefer to have the final say about things...."

Letting my remark pass, he emptied his glass. "I'll brief Rose and then immediately get the money together. Keep me posted on the day, time, and location of everything." Suddenly, he started rat-a-tat-tatting out some more laughs. "Regarding your movie review, I totally agree. You couldn't pay me to see another Viogram picture. Now, shall we order more drinks?"

I doubted if I could have paid him to do anything. It would have cost me more money than I've ever made or ever would make.

The next day, Sara and I killed a couple pots of her coffee and a pack of my cigarettes, talking about Viogram's demand for ransom and how to pull off the transfer. I wanted to hand them the money across the busy street from one of LA's two Bullock's department stores. The question was: which one?

Sara argued for the now more famed Bullock's on Wilshire Boulevard. It was a striking beige and green Art Deco building with a tower that beamed out a violet light. The block-long store attracted a lot of traffic, but not the kind I wanted.

Because this part of LA was more suburban-like, there were cars everywhere but few pedestrians. It wasn't crowded enough for me.

I preferred the Bullock's downtown on Seventh and Broadway. This older building didn't stand out like the Bullocks on Wilshire, but it was taller and longer and sat in a part of town that was swamped with both cars and people. The neighborhood seemed an ideal place to transfer so much money anonymously yet safely. Or so I thought. I was going downtown to shop for Julie's freedom.

Chapter Fourteen

After working out a plan and reviewing it with Greenstein, I called Pittman the next day to make arrangements for the transfer. Jeannie answered.

"Hello, this is Mr. Pittman's office."

"Hi, sweetheart, this is Matt."

"Matt?" Her voice became a nervous whisper. "How are you? Why are you calling me here?"

"I'm not. I'm actually trying to reach your boss. We're supposed to make arrangements for Julie's release. It involves money, of course."

"A ransom?"

"Yeah, but you shouldn't be talking about it."

"Will it be dangerous?"

"We'll see. Is he around?"

"Yes, I'll connect you. Please be careful, Matt." She was a sweet kid, and I hoped she wouldn't get dragged into this case any further.

Almost a minute later, Pittman found his way to the phone. "Yeah, Moulton?" He grumbled.

"I'm calling to give you the details on the transfer."

"You're giving *me* the details?"

"That's right. Morgan agreed that I would set the terms."

There was a harrumph. "Okay," he said, with reluctance.

I talked slowly and deliberately. "The transfer should happen tomorrow afternoon at 3:00. I'll be standing downtown at the traffic light on Seventh Avenue facing the Bullock's department store across the street on Broadway."

"But it's so crowded there." Pittman apparently wasn't the brightest of corporate crooks.

"Yeah, becoming lost in the crowd is the whole point. I'll be standing there in a light gray suit and matching fedora. I'll be holding a brown Bullock's shopping bag with $25,000 in old hundred-dollar bills. The money will be hidden under fancy red tissue paper. Are you getting all this down?"

"Yes, of course," he said in a rushed voice. He didn't sound as if he had much experience taking his own notes.

"Now, I have to be able to properly identify the guy you send to pick up the money. I don't care about the color of his suit, but he should be wearing a beige fedora with a black band and—this is really important—he should be sporting a black eye patch. It doesn't matter which eye the patch covers."

"A beige fedora with a black band? A black eye patch? Where am I supposed to find these things at the last minute?"

"I guess you didn't realize this, but you work for a film studio, Pittman. You have a props department that must be full of hats and eye patches. You could dress a mug for work every day in that place."

There was a noisy silence. It sounded as if he was stewing.

"Now, your guy should also be carrying a brown Bullock's shopping bag stuffed with something covered by tissue paper. At 3:00, he should cross the intersection at Seventh, approaching from the Bullock's side of the street. Once he reaches me, he should put his bag down and bend over to tie his shoe or pick up something he dropped, like a coin. He then should take my Bullock's bag, and I'll take his, and we'll proceed to go our own separate ways. Is all that clear? Do you have any questions?"

"What happens if there are a lot of police around?"

"So what? Why should that bother us? What do they have to be suspicious of? Our having shopped at Bullock's? A guy stopping to tie his shoe? I don't understand what you're getting at, Pittman."

"I'm just trying to be careful," he said in a resentful tone.

"Okay, now comes the most crucial part. When and how do I get Julie?"

"Ah, well, first we have to take the money back and count it. Make sure it's not marked. If everything's okay, we'll call you to come pick her up at our Beverly Hills location."

"No, no, that's too dangerous. We may never get out of there. You guys will have to drop her off the next day at the same time, and the same place downtown. I'll be standing there wearing the same clothes, holding that Bullock's bag you left me." I raised my voice. "And you must keep your part of the bargain. If you don't produce Julie, I'll start singing to anyone who will listen—the police, the press, the DA. I'm no Sinatra, but my voice will carry. Are we in agreement on all this?"

It took him forever to respond. "Yes…."

"Any questions?" I worried about confusion and caprice. And then there was the unknown.

"No. It's all clear to me."

Actually, the next day wasn't clear at all. The sky was so darkly overcast that it seemed to cast a shadow on the downtown shoppers. But the threat of rain didn't deter the LA crowds. They would shop even if they knew that German or

Japanese soldiers were closing in from the suburbs. After all, there were stars to see, products to buy, sales to beat. Too much was at stake to give up shopping for any reason, much less the weather. The possibility of rain did concern me, however. I didn't want to be lugging around a waterlogged bag of cash that might tear or even collapse. At this point, I needed luck, a better weather forecast, or probably both.

I was early. It was about ten minutes to three, and so I window-shopped on Seventh, a few doors down from the intersection with Broadway. I looked into a jewelry store and saw counters full of pricey rings, necklaces, and bracelets, but I couldn't keep my eyes off the richest item: a gorgeous redheaded doll whose boyfriend, lover, or husband was apparently about to buy her something. I wondered how much it was going to cost. Love could be a very expensive affair—and the price wasn't always money.

It was now three minutes to three, and so I headed to the intersection. I wanted to be there early in case my trading partner's watch was running fast. The light changed a couple of times, and suddenly it was three o'clock. Okay, where was he? People gathered around me at the red light. When it changed, they walked forward, and I remained. Meanwhile, pedestrians approached me from the other side of the street, but my eye-patched contact wasn't among them. That happened a few more times, and now it was a quarter after three. He was very late. Where was he? It already seemed as if I had been waiting on this corner for an eternity. I scanned the block across the street, and all I saw were people and more people, but no one resembling my contact. Ironically however, they all looked a little suspicious, self-consciously eyeing one another, searching—no doubt—for the possible star hiding among them.

Five minutes passed, then five minutes more. Should I abandon the wait? Five minutes later, at 3:30, I scanned the block across the street again and finally spotted my man with the hat, the eye patch, and the Bullock's bag. But he was standing still, looking with grave concern down Broadway. Did he think he was being followed? All I could do was wait a little longer.

A minute later, he disappeared, seemingly swallowed up by a new wave of people. Should I wait a while longer and give him the chance to shake his tail, if that's what the problem had been? A few more minutes passed, and a bedraggled beggar approached me holding his hat out. "Spare change, sir?" I tried to ignore him so that I could concentrate on the intersection and the block across the street. But he wouldn't let me do it. He was like the neighborhood dog that wouldn't stop barking. "Spare change, sir? Spare change? Spare change?" I finally pulled a dollar from my wallet and threw it into his hat. "Oh, thank you, sir, thank you."

"Okay, shove off, friend," I bellowed. The march of people continued, but still no patch man. I was waiting to give ransom money away, but there was still no taker.

At 3:45, I decided to end the wait: The light was red, but I didn't see my patch man among the pedestrians on the other side of the street. I looked to my left at the pedestrians crossing Broadway, and—wait—my contact was walking among them. He was crossing the wrong street. So I turned to face his direction. We could make the bag exchange in a few seconds, as soon as he had gradually reached the curb. There was a young woman walking behind him, but—seemingly out of nowhere—a tall guy in a dark suit and hat rushed over, pushed her aside, and punched my contact in the back. Patch man slowly staggered across the street and then collapsed, face first, with his bag in hand, at my feet. There was a knife sticking out of his back. Two women were screaming. A guy was calling out for the police. Everybody was gathering around. I turned and quickly walked the other way, across Seventh. I couldn't get caught in that bloody mess with a bag of money in my hands. The skies rumbled and the rain began to fall hard. By the time I reached my car, I was soaking wet, but I didn't know whether it was primarily from the rain or my own sweat. I drove out of there. So much for careful planning.

I rushed into the office, passing Sara without so much as a nod.

"Hi Matt…. Oh, what's wrong?"

I went into my inner office, discarded my jacket, poured a long drink, and quaffed it down. I then opened my safe and started stuffing it with the ransom money.

Sara came in on me. "Oh, no. The transfer didn't happen…."

"No, it died on Seventh. Somebody didn't want Viogram to get the money, Julie to be released, or both. So they stabbed my contact in the back before he could reach me."

I closed the safe and poured myself another long whisky.

"Did you get a make on the assailant?" She asked with eyebrows raised.

"Not really. The day was dark, and he was darker, shadowed by a large hat."

"Who do you think did it? Rose Fischetti's mob antagonists?" Her arms were crossed, and a cigarette dangled from her mouth.

"That idea occurred to me. But now I don't think it makes any sense. If it were Rose's enemies, wouldn't they rather wait and then kill or kidnap Julie themselves?" I killed the second drink.

"What about your enemies…from San Francisco?'

I walked over to my desk and sat down. "No, why would they kill my contact? They would've killed me. And they wouldn't have had to do it there, in public. They could've killed me anytime in private, here in the office, or at home in my bed."

"That's right—that was a stupid question." She lowered her eyes and folded her hands together as if she was now molding a better one.

"No, it wasn't, sweetheart. I thought about that idea, too." I lit a much-needed smoke.

"What's your best guess now, Matt?'

"I'm starting to think that it was an internal job, that someone within Viogram didn't want this transfer to happen."

"Could that someone be Pittman?" She walked toward me and sat down in the client chair.

"Yes, Pittman, as the cops say, is my main suspect. He knew all the details about the transfer, but he may not have liked the idea of giving up his best escort. He may not have appreciated Morgan interfering in his Entertainment Services business. It could even be that Pittman has designs on Morgan's job. If he arranged to botch the transfer, that would make Morgan look bad. But it's all just speculation."

"It sounds like a great guess based on the limited information we have."

"Yeah, but how great is it? Reality may have another idea." After we looked into space for a few minutes—and space didn't answer—I stood up and slipped into my wet jacket. "I'm going home to think this over." I bent down to kiss her forehead. "Thanks for being such a good dick, sweetheart."

Later, at home, I wanted to put the Julie Fischetti case to

rest for a while, and so I sat back and listened to some of my favorite records. This was going to be Nat King Cole night. As I lost myself in his bluesy "Mona Lisa" song, the phone rang. I was tempted to just let it ring, but I thought I better not give in to temptation—this time.

"Hello."

"Oh, Matt, it's Jeannie."

"How are you, doll?"

"I should be asking you that. I gather that the money exchange ended up in disaster for you."

"How'd you know that?"

"Pittman was acting extremely agitated during two calls he took late this afternoon. It wasn't clear what he was talking about, but I could tell that it was about something really big. And then I saw the headline story in the evening paper about the guy who was stabbed to death on a downtown street. It even had a picture of his face. Was he your contact?"

"Yes, he was. He was supposed to take the ransom off my hands, but he never quite made it. Someone made sure of that."

"Who?"

"That's the question of the hour. But I'd take short odds that someone inside Viogram arranged the hit."

"Oh, my God! I thought I was working for a company whose business was make-believe, not the bloody real thing."

"Tell that to your bosses. I think those people take themselves way too seriously. They're ready to do anything for the bottom line. And that's why you may be in danger—they've connected you to troublemaking me. After our evening together, a guy followed me to the neighborhood diner and tried to choke the life out of me. I suspect that he had been trailing you and then us all evening."

"Goodness no!" Her voice shuddered. "What's wrong with these people?"

"They're people, except more so—and that's the worst kind. But forget about that, just worry about yourself. Never call me from your office: Someone may be listening."

"Matt, I'm scared for me, and I'm scared for you."

"Well, that's a good thing—a scared person is usually a careful person. But doll, you mentioned before about Pittman's incoherence on the phone this afternoon. Did he say anything that made any sense at all?"

"Hmm, it was all so disjointed. He kept saying 'no,' 'you sure,' and 'how could that happen.' It was a bunch of confused reactions. But...wait, I'm trying to remember that one line—it was so chilling. Oh yeah, he said, 'she should have killed him instead.' I don't know what he meant by that."

"He said 'she'—'she should have killed him instead'?"

"Yes...."

"It was he who killed my contact. Pittman must have been talking about the person who ordered the hit. My insider looks to be a she."

"Who's the 'him' she should have killed?"

I laughed. "That's yours truly. Pittman doesn't like me. I caused him trouble about his sex slavery business, and I took away his girl."

She begged my pardon, in so many words. "I've never dated that creep!"

"That doesn't matter. He may still think of you as his girl. In my business, I've seen a lot of men—and women, for that matter—get violently possessive over someone or something they *didn't* really have. That's just another reason why you have to be careful here."

"Matt, why do you keep trying to open up my eyes to things?" She said in a playfully sarcastic tone. King's "Orange Colored Sky" was playing in the background.

"Because I like you. I'm just trying to help you see the world as it really is. Hell, I'm still learning how to do that myself."

"What does helping me see have to do with my feet?" She asked coyly.

"Frankly, I don't know. But I had to start somewhere, didn't I? I went feet first—and oh what feet!"

She just laughed.

"Sweetheart, I love the sound of your voice, but I have to go now. With Pittman's "she" line, you've given me much more to think about. Watch your step, and call me at home if you need to talk."

"Oh, okay," she said, sounding as if she wished she had more to say. "Be careful, Matt. Good night…."

Jeannie got my mind working again. If the foiling of the ransom transfer really was an inside job, and the perpetrator really was a she, who could be a more powerful and influential suspect than the Chairman of the Board of Directors herself, Ruth Gettling Baines? I called her office the next morning and arranged a meeting.

Chapter Fifteen

M rs. Baines kept her chairman's office in the thirteen-story General Petroleum Building, a brand-new, all-steel structure on Flower Street. Her steel-magnate dad would have been proud. But I wondered what her independent-minded, film-pioneer husband would have made of it. The building was imposing, but in a blocky, regimentally corporate kind of way. The vertically arranged shutters, its one distinctive feature, redirected the heat away from the windows, but that meant they redirected the light and the outside life away as well. It was a movie company sealed and buried in an oil building. While it was just the single office, the anti-corporate Mr. Baines would probably have seen Viogram's presence there as a real outrage.

However, his wife's outer office differed significantly from the offices in the current corporate studio. It not only acknowledged Viogram's business, it celebrated it as well. Framed movie posters and signed star photos hung all around— the place looked like a little Viogram museum. I took it all in like a sightseeing tourist, as I cased the joint like a diligent dick. A unique half wall divided two desks. At one sat a bespectacled young brunette woman with a long face that seemed to be contemplating the next business deal. The other desk accommodated a bored, slack-jawed, black-haired heavy of thirty or so who looked as if his only business was trouble. I had seen him somewhere before, but my memory refused to provide a match. When he noticed I was staring at him, he quickly lowered his ink-black eyes to study the playing cards he was shuffling on his desk. He sat in front of a double-door, as did the young woman. They were probably separate entrances to Ruth Gettling Baines's larger office. One side for business, one side for unpleasantness.

My mind was still in the clouds, searching for cards man when the secretary spoke up and brought me back down to earth.

"May I help you, sir?" she asked, in her nine-to-five voice

I removed my black fedora. "I have an appointment with Mrs. Baines. Matt Moulton's the name."

"She's running a little late. Please have a seat, Mr. Moulton."

She was running very late. A half hour passed before four older men in pricey pinstripe suits emerged from her office. They looked tired, as if they had just labored through a Board of Directors' meeting. The rich had it so very tough—as tough as filet mignon, cooked medium rare.

"Okay, Mrs. Baines will see you now, Mr. Moulton."

I walked into her cavernous office and discovered life—lots of it. More of the most dramatic film posters decorated the room, and fresh flowers appeared here, there, and everywhere, even on the modernistic conference table. The bare walls showed personality, too, painted in a dusty rose color that contrasted with the plush navy-blue carpeting. Mrs. Baines herself was a study in contrasts. The handsome woman, now sporting streaked blonde hair, was enthusiastically dressed for big business in a smart, shapely—but not too shapely—brown skirt suit. But her weary lost-in the-wilderness expression—though leavened somewhat by eager-to-please smiles—conveyed ambivalence, confusion, and a general desperation.

"How do you do, Mr. Moulton? I'm so pleased to make your acquaintance. Please take a seat," she said, as her open, outstretched hand seemed to introduce me to the felt navy blue chair that sat in front of her desk. She then lowered herself into her own seat in a ceremonial manner, as if she were readying to lead the board again.

"I'm so excited to be in the presence of a real private investigator," she said with an odd breathlessness. "My only experience with private eyes has been through books and movies. Is your life as dramatic as they make it out to be in fiction?"

"Dramatic?" I laughed. "I guess it might be to someone watching things from the outside. To me, it's a job. It's often very interesting, but sometimes it's very dangerous. Like this one has been. Mind if I smoke?"

"Oh, please do, Mr. Moulton." She looked up and away, as if she were staring at a screen. "I've so enjoyed those detective stories, particularly the ones on film." She then smiled at me. "I will admit to you that our main competitor, RKO, made my favorite movie of the bunch, 'Murder My Sweet.' Did you see that picture, Mr. Moulton?"

"Yes, I liked it, but I found it totally unrealistic."

"Really? Don't personal betrayals and murders happen in your business?" Her voice began to falter before she finished.

"Oh, of course they do. The story of 'Murder My Sweet' is very plausible. What's unrealistic is wasting a talented song-and-dance man like Dick Powell in the serious role of the dick. Gumshoes don't have any big talents, and don't really need them, to be frank. All they have to be able to do is ask questions, solve puzzles, and be a relentless pain-in-the-ass. Please excuse my French, Mrs. Baines, but that's what I am, a pain-in-the-ass—I don't give up easily."

She laughed nervously. "I'm sure you're more talented than you're giving yourself credit for, Mr. Moulton. Regarding Powell, he just did what good actors do: pretend to tell the truth." I gathered she wasn't talking about Powell and movie acting.

I took a long drag on my smoke. "Well, I love Powell and the pictures, but that's not what I've come to talk to you about, Mrs. Baines."

"I know. I'm sorry. I often fall into reveries about the movies. They bring back such wonderful memories of my husband George, who loved me...." Something seemed to get caught in her throat. "...and loved the movies. I never appreciated him enough when he was around. Never. I remember when we first met, in a movie theater in San Francisco...."

That's it—it was San Francisco! I remember now: I encountered Card Man when I was starting out in the Frisco City Detective Bureau. The cops brought in this punk who they suspected was working as a close assistant to a wanted mob figure and stone-cold killer. They put a little bit of a squeeze on the punk, and he knuckled under completely, revealing all kinds of secrets about his boss, almost down to the brand of toilet paper he used. The DA later released the snitch, uncharged, for his "cooperation." So now he's working for Mrs. Baines. It seems like everyone comes to Hollywood eventually....

"It wasn't until our third movie date that George revealed he owned a film studio...."

I hoped I hadn't missed anything important when my mind wandered into the dark. "Mrs. Baines, I respect George Baines and his role in the development of movies. Furthermore, the story of your relationship is very interesting, and it certainly helps me fill in the overall picture of things. But honestly, Mr. Baines is not my main concern. I'm here about another matter. I represent a client who…."

"Yes, yes, I know Mr. Moulton." She took the pitcher on her desk, poured herself a full glass of water, and slowly drank it down. "I've read that water is very healthy for you. Would you like a glass?" Her face smiled, but her mouth didn't move.

Here we go on another tangent. "No thanks, Mrs. Baines. I take in my healthy water through whisky, coffee, and an occasional Coke during the hot weather. But now please…."

"Yes, I know Mr. Moulton," she said with some exasperation, "you're here looking for that colored actress, Julie Fischetti."

I felt as if we had just struck gold. "Yes, exactly. Now let me tell you what I've found…."

"I know the whole story already." She looked down at her desk. "I've been struggling with this matter for weeks, months. Sometimes it seems like years." She seemed to age before my eyes.

"Then you know your company is running a black-sex slavery operation?"

"Yes, I'm aware of the sex business, and I've been totally opposed to it. It's immoral, and it's got nothing to do with movies. But slavery, Mr. Moulton? Isn't that a bit of an exaggeration?"

"It's forced labor and confinement, Mrs. Baines. Wouldn't you call that slavery? If you have a better word, I'll consider it." I mashed out my cigarette in her rose-colored ashtray.

"Whatever you call it, it wasn't part of our original dream."

"Whose dream, Mrs. Baines? Are you talking about your and your husband's?"

She looked away. "It wasn't part of the promise," she said, seemingly to herself. Then she returned to the present and looked at me. "I apologize for my incoherence, Mr. Moulton. I really want to focus on...helping you. But I feel so... overwhelmed. It's been such a long day, such a long week...."

Just as Mrs. Baines started to open up, her secretary entered the room to close things down. "Excuse me, Mrs. Baines, your call has just come in," she said, with a telephone operator's officiousness. While I didn't think the interruption was intentional, it sure looked suspicious: The secretary couldn't have picked a better time to relieve her boss.

"Oh, thank you, Beth, I'll take it right now. Mr. Moulton, could we talk about your Julie later...over dinner tonight? We'll go to Ciro's, my favorite place in the whole world."

Another see-and-be-seen Hollywood haunt on Sunset Boulevard. "Okay, but you have to assure me that we're going to talk business—my client's business."

"I'll make that a vow." She raised her drawn eyebrows to punctuate the remark. She then wrote her address on the back of a business card. "Please come by at seven—I'll make our dinner reservations for 8:00." Her eyes seemed to be begging me to leave her alone right now. "Thank you, Mr. Moulton— see you then."

On my way out, I stole another glance at Card Man. The mob double-crosser was still hard at work over a game of solitaire. And he still didn't want to look my way.

Mrs. Baines also dwelt in Beverly Hills, on Broad Beach Road. Although her wealth dwarfed that of almost anyone else in Hollywood, she lived in a two-story brown-gray mansion that was almost modest in comparison with the neighboring homes, including Viogram's sex plantation. Surrounded by a lot of green—overgrown grass and jungle-like bushes—the place was impressive in an almost unkempt way. You had to appreciate the wild side it exposed.

It was a much tamer animal inside. The rooms were self-consciously open and airy, as if someone—probably Mrs. Baines's designer—spent more to do less, and all in mostly neutral colors. The style had a name—minimalism—and it had a purpose: To show everybody that she was one of the tasteful rich, one of those who didn't have to openly scream out her wealth. Probably only the filthy rich—someone like Mrs. Baines—could afford a style that was so self-consciously clean.

The lady of the house and I sat around in this environment for a half-hour drinking her old fashioneds. A sugary cocktail wasn't my kind of drink, but she loved it, and I wanted to do whatever I could to win her over to my cause of freeing Julie. She kept reminiscing about her husband and the old film business, and I let her talk, thinking that we'd take up my matter at dinner in Ciro's. Besides, her chatter proved unexpectedly revealing. She seemed to painfully regret some things she did or didn't do. What were they, and would they be important to this case? Finally, it was time to go, and she rang for the butler. A short, bald gentleman, with an informal manner, showed up in seconds.

"What do you need, Mrs. Baines?" asked the butler, in an accent that sounded as if it was from Brooklyn. Perhaps the man had once worked for the Gettling family on the East Coast.

"James, would you tell Garth to get the car? We're ready to

leave."

"You got it, ma'am."

James returned a minute later. "I'm sorry, Mrs. Baines: Garth isn't around. Mildred said he left a couple of hours ago without leaving a word."

Mrs. Baines reacted as if James had just slapped her in the face. "What? That's not acceptable." Her voice got real high-pitched. "I talked with him again and again about tonight. He knows I like to take the caddie when I go to Ciro's. But I wanted him to drive us there."

She went to the phone and dialed. "That's okay, James, I'll call him at home." I heard Garth's phone ring, and ring, and ring. Mrs. Baines finally slammed the receiver done in disgust. "Where could he be?"

"Mrs. Baines, is Garth the young man who sits and does nothing at a desk in front of your office?"

She was pouring herself a whisky, this time without the extras. "Yes, he does nothing there. But he fills an important role as my assistant, a kind of chauffeur and bodyguard, and oh—I don't know—overall troubleshooter. He's ordinarily so reliable."

"You find yourself needing a bodyguard?"

"You never know when you need one. His presence helps make me feel secure." She sipped her bourbon with a faraway, thoughtful look. "Well, I'll drive us to Ciro's myself."

So the double-crosser suddenly disappears. Without a word. I was starting to think paranoid thoughts, and I decided that I better take them seriously. "Mrs. Baines, do you mind if we're a little late?"

"No, why?"

"I need to give somebody a call." I dialed the phone. Within seconds, my party answered. "Hello, Vito? Wow—you're answering phones now? This is Matt Moulton. I'm fine. And yourself? Good...good. Now listen, Vito, I'm in a potentially tough spot, and I need your help. Are you available to come see me right now? There's $100 in it for you. No, I'm in Beverly Hills, on Broad Beach Road." I gave him the address, and he told me he'd drive over as soon as possible.

"What's this all about, Mr. Moulton? Who is Vito?" She walked over and—empty glass in hand—confronted me with her confusion.

"He's someone whose presence will help make *me* feel secure."

Unshaven, droopy-eyed Vito Pacino arrived straight from work, wearing his usual worn blue jeans, oil-stained blue shirt, and ratty baseball cap. He was a 40-year-old grease monkey— and a highly successful one at that. He not only owned and managed five busy auto-repair shops but also continued doing a lot of the most challenging mechanical jobs there. He loved cars too much to completely give up the garage for the front office. He also loved his wife, and that's where I had originally come in.

Vito thought that there had to be an innocent and respectable reason why she was so seldom at home anymore. He hired me to investigate, and I discovered the real reason—a handsome deadbeat friend. She was screwing the guy and providing his means of support. Okay, if you wanted to see things from her side, you could say she was a charitable soul who needed a little more exercise. But there was only one way to see the gun she had bought her lover and the personal information about her husband she had provided him: She wanted Vito's money, without Vito attached. His wife would never have gotten away with it, but that wouldn't have been any solace to a dead Vito.

When I broke the news to him, I broke his heart. But I also made a grateful friend who felt he owed his life to me.

"Vito, I'm sorry to drag you all the way out here. First, I'd like you to meet Mrs. Baines." He greeted her, but all she could do in return was tip her head in acknowledgement and struggle to close her wide-open mouth.

"Mrs. Baines, would you show us to your caddie?"

"My caddie? Okay, but why?" She was still at a loss about what was going on.

She took us to her beloved Cadillac. It was whiter than white and unusually shiny, creating a new color that I would have called radioactive snow.

"Vito, I'm worried about this car. I feel it might have an unexpected extra—something added long after the showroom, perhaps as recently as today."

"Like what, Matt?"

"Like a bomb."

Vito's eyes widened, but he otherwise took my idea in stride. "Oh sure, Matt, I'll look over the car for you."

Mrs. Baines was another story. She seemed both seized and defiant, as if she was arguing with a heart attack. "Oh, come now, Mr. Moulton. A bomb? Why?" she asked while gasping for breath.

"I could be wrong. We'll see."

Mrs. Baines and I went back into the house and drank and smoked in silence. I felt almost as jittery as she looked. Was this going to be the third attempt on my life in just days?

A little while later, the butler brought back Vito with the truth: He gingerly held in his two hands a metallic device that looked like a turtle shell with wires.

"Matt, you were right: There was a bomb in the car, and it

looks pretty sophisticated. I'm no expert, but I think this thing would have blown the caddie to kingdom come." He couldn't stop shaking his head.

Mrs. Baines let out a suppressed scream. I couldn't give voice to my feelings, because they were a confusing mix of anger, fear, and cold relief. I was luckier than I thought.

"Would just starting the car have set off the bomb?"

"No, Matt, it wasn't connected that way. It wouldn't have gone off until you picked up some speed."

"Guess what, Mrs. Baines? We would never have made it to Ciro's." She didn't seem to know what to say or do or where to go, and so she just teetered over to the bar to pour another drink. She forgot she had guests.

"Thanks Vito, you saved our lives." I pulled a hundred-dollar bill from my wallet and tried to give it to him.

He waved it off and smiled. "Call us even now, Matt. I'm just happy I could help you." After putting the bomb down gently on the table, he opened his mouth to say something, paused as if to reconsider, and then seemed to come up with something more urgent. "What kind of crazy world are we living in, Matt?"

"That's what I ask myself almost every day—and I never get an answer. And I never will… Would you like Mrs. Baines to mix you a drink?"

"No thanks, Matt. I have to go."

I grabbed his arm and shook his hand. "Well, the next time we get together, I'm buying you dinner and drinks. Is that clear?"

He smiled. "I can see it and taste it now, Matt. Bye-bye."

I didn't wait for her to offer me a drink—I went right to the bar and poured my own. There was a lot of good liquor there.

"Okay, Mrs. Baines, it's time for an honest talk. What's going on in this company? It looks like there's a civil war. What are you guys battling over? Viogram's system of slavery? It's out of control."

She started to falter again. "Civil war? I wouldn't go that far...."

"Oh, c'mon Mrs. Baines. Open your eyes: The other side wanted to kill you tonight, and I was going to be their bonus victim. It was the third time they tried to eliminate me, but let's put that aside for now. They retaliated against you for what you did yesterday afternoon to their ransom collection guy. Why did your order his murder?"

She stood there, in her sleek black gown with silver spackles, with the empty lipstick-stained glass pressed against her mouth, pondering how to deflect my question. "Murder, why do you have to use such overpowering words?"

"Because it was murder. Why'd you order it? Why wouldn't you just let the guy take my client's ransom payment?"

She sat down on the sofa and put the empty glass on the coffee table. "I didn't want anyone murdered—I just wanted to stop the illicit money transfer. Put an end to the prostitution and the bribery. Make the company a respectable business again—a real film company, like George intended."

"Bribery? Who is Viogram bribing?"

"The Beverly Hills Police. And the Los Angeles County Police. And the local politicians." She laughed, with a sad look. "They're bribing the same politicians who regularly buy time with the escorts."

"Who are 'they,' Mrs. Baines?"

She looked off in the distance, opened her thin-lipped mouth, and said...nothing.

I sat down in the chair across from her. "Who are 'they'? I assume that 'they' are led by Spencer Morgan?" I needed to light a smoke, but I didn't want to interrupt the momentum, break my concentration.

Her eyes dropped, and her face tightened. "Yes....he was the person who called this afternoon. I tried to reason with him about the escort stuff."

"Reason with him? I don't understand you, Mrs. Baines. You say you were disturbed over the disreputable direction of the business. Well then, why didn't you take direct action? As the Chairman of the Board of Directors, you could've fired Morgan. Why didn't you do it?"

She wanted to put some daylight—or at least some smoke—between my question and her answer, and so she paused to light a cigarette and take a long drag. "I tried, Mr. Moulton. I tried to talk to him about what he and Pittman were doing to hurt the company. But he just wouldn't listen. He was determined to do what he wanted, what he thought was most profitable, legal or not."

"Okay, but you're his boss. So now, why don't you fire him?"

She shook her head and blew more smoke.

"Is the reason you won't fire him an intimate one? Are you or were you romantically involved with him?"

For the first time in our acquaintance, her face flashed mean—less a hot mean than a more cold-blooded one. "Who are you to ask me a question as personal as that?"

"Who am I? I'm the dick who's trying to free my client's daughter from slavery and forced dope addiction. Is that a good enough answer for you, Mrs. Baines? Or should I rephrase the truth?"

Her expression returned to a more neutral version of troubled. "I'm sorry, Mr. Moulton. I didn't mean to offend you. I lost my temper at the wrong person."

I stood up and lit a much-needed cigarette. "Well, who's the right person? Spencer Morgan? I still don't think you realize that someone from the other side—Morgan's side—tried to blow you up tonight. Doesn't that scare or at least bother you?"

She seemed lost in thought, with an expression that looked more anguished than scared. Then, that flash of mean returned, and I knew that I wasn't the target this time. She remained quiet for a while, and then she said, "I've got to finally do something about this whole affair, I mean this whole nasty business," she said slowly. "We should meet with Spencer tonight."

"Would you be able to arrange a meeting on such short notice?"

"I don't care about the short notice. He has to make himself available tonight. Now. And he has to release that woman, your Julie Fischetti." Her gown had a provocative slit in the lower front, and so when she carelessly uncrossed her legs, she ended up exposing a lot of upper thigh and more. It was a nice view. But it probably wasn't intentional: She was looking without seeing. She was dead focused on her immediate future with Morgan—the big meeting.

"Where should we meet him, Mrs. Baines?"

"It needs to happen at the mansion."

"I warn you that that's a dangerous place. Are you willing to take the risk?"

"Spencer does everything indirectly, on the sly. He wouldn't move against us there." She stood up. "If you'll excuse me, I'm going to go make the arrangements." She seemed to sleepwalk out of the room. Even in her fuzzy, focused state, she was self-aware enough to insist that the fateful call to Morgan be a private one. But the whole affair, the whole case, wouldn't stay private for much longer.

Now, if I could only keep myself and my client's daughter alive….

Chapter Sixteen

Mrs. Baines's call put the world on edge—at least the world of Viogram and its plantation in Beverly Hills. It was darker than night there: Somebody turned off all the outside lights, apparently closing the escort business for the meeting. Mrs. Baines and I found our way to the door, but I was surprised to see who answered our ring. It wasn't the butler, it was the surly, self-important corporate pimp, Ralph Norton.

"Welcome, Mrs. Baines—please come right in. Mr. Morgan just arrived a few minutes ago. He's waiting for you in the library."

Norton didn't even address me, unless you considered the hard look he threw my way. As he escorted us to the library, I counted the roving presence of three thugs. What I wanted to know was how many more were lurking in the shadows? Norton directed us into the library, where a sitting Morgan rose from his chair and rushed over to Mrs. Baines.

"Ruth, how are you?" he asked, with his stilted smile. Morgan wore a silk blue jacket with a white cashmere muffler, instead of a tie. He looked like an actor playing a rich playboy in a bad "B" movie. "It's been too long since we've last seen each other." He grabbed her hands and tried to hold them.

She pulled away, looked down at the floor, and said: "Yes, it's been a while."

Norton apparently had had his boys redecorate this part of the library. They arranged three chairs facing each other in a half circle. A small table/desk with an ashtray sat by each chair. It looked as if they were expecting a Roosevelt-Churchill-Stalin kind of summit. What was my negotiating strategy? Arranging a peace that would last long enough for Julie and I to safely get the Hell out of that place.

I took the chair that faced the door: I wanted to make sure I could see who was coming in and going out. Mrs. Baines sat to my right, and Morgan sat directly across from me. Norton asked us what we wanted to drink. Mrs. Baines opted for a whisky sour, and I chose bourbon on the rocks. Meanwhile, it looked like Morgan was drinking his beloved Glenfiddich. Once we were all set with our drinks, Norton finally left. His departure could brighten any room, or so it seemed to me.

"Now, tell me, why the need for this emergency meeting?" Morgan asked, with his hands spread out wide.

"Oh, c'mon Spencer, you know why I had to come here tonight," she said through gritted teeth. "It's time to end this Julie Fischetti matter. I told you long ago that this entertainment escort service was wrong, and that it was going to cause us trouble one day."

"What do you mean end the Julie Fischetti matter? She's a Viogram player bound by a contract," he said, trying, and essentially failing, to smile.

"I mean tear up the contract—let her go," she said, with utter exasperation. I had a feeling that that was the first time Mrs. Baines had truly been firm with her executive leader/lover. This was going to be an interesting show, and I lit a cigarette to better enjoy it.

He chuckled at the order and subtly taunted her. "Are you now the chief executive of Viogram?"

"No, but I lead the Board that oversees you and your unsavory activities."

"So what does that mean?" He sipped his scotch with assurance.

"It means, it means....I could ask the Board to fire you."

Her impertinence began to anger him. "How could you do that after all I've done for the company? It's more profitable than ever before. The future promises even more growth."

"Yes, but we were once a real film company, George's film company. And now I don't know what we are. You've turned Viogram into a rank, immoral, corporate circus."

"It sounds as if you've been spending too much time with Mr. Moulton here."

She was leaning over the chair in his direction. "I have my own eyes and ears—I can see and hear what's going on without his help. All he did was fill in some of the details of this sorry story."

"So now what, my dear?" It was hard to see how she could ever have been charmed by his confident emptiness.

"Spencer, you desperately wanted to lead a corporation, and now you're doing it. But remember, you don't own the place. Just like every other corporate chief executive, you have to follow rules: The Chairman of the Board is ordering you to do something that's for the good of the company."

"I've never known you to care much for the coloreds. That isn't the problem, is it?"

The only answer he got back from her was a determined scowl. Then he looked at me, and I was silent, too. He sighed and shook his head, stood up, and walked to the phone, then dialed and waited. "Norton, would you come to the library, please?"

A drag on my smoke and a passing thought later, the pimp was at the door. "Yes, Mr. Morgan?"

"We're letting Miss Fischetti go. Help the young woman pack her things and then bring her to the library. She'll be leaving with Mr. Moulton." Morgan couldn't admit that he was releasing her from bondage. Instead, he was 'letting her go"—firing her.

Norton just stood there with a bewildered, oddly begrudging look. "But Mr. Morgan…."

"But what, Norton!?" he said, his voice raised. "Are you going to give me a hard time as well?"

"No, sir. I'll get her ready right away." He slithered out.

Morgan finished his glass of scotch. "Ruth, I just don't know what happened to you. We had such a close relationship… business-wise. But all that changed the other afternoon downtown…."

She crossed her arms and turned up the volume. "What are you accusing me of? And what about what you tried to pull off tonight?"

"Mrs. Baines, please hold it right there a moment," I requested. "I'd like to honor Mr. Morgan with this gift, which marks the event to which you referred." I walked over to Morgan and handed him the cardboard box I had been carrying.

He didn't know how to react, and so he became very uncomfortable. I heard him mumble "what the Hell" and then he removed the top of the box and saw his gift. "What is it?"

"It's the bomb your thugs attached to Mrs. Baines's car late this afternoon or early this evening." He was so paralyzed that even fear couldn't emerge on his face. "Thank you, Morgan, but it turns out we couldn't use it. Perhaps you could give it to another business colleague or loved one."

"Now you're accusing me of attempted murder? Is that just more of your theatrics?" It seemed to take him almost a minute to move the box three feet over to the side table.

"Morgan, tonight might have been your first attempt on Mrs. Baines's life. But it was your third attempt on mine. I don't appreciate that. And you know what? I don't like your entertainment slavery service either. I was originally going to forget about it and instead focus on getting my client's daughter back. But now that's not enough for me—you'll have to do more than just release Julie. Whether my client likes the idea or not, I will go public with the Viogram slavery story if you don't release everyone tonight. I'm just being honest with you. And now I want both of you to be honest with me." Morgan was giving me a look of daggers throughout my spiel. But now Mrs. Baines looked up at me as well, and her expression was one of worry.

"Whose idea was it to kill George Baines?"

Mrs. Baines' head dropped, and she let out a short, shivering sob—it was as if she had just been sliced open and this was her dying sound.

Morgan thought he had an answer for everything, and this question was no exception. "What are you trying to imply? George Baines died of diabetes."

"Well, I'm not a doctor—and neither are you, Morgan. But diabetes is a disorder characterized by too much sugar in the blood. A diabetic has to inject insulin to reduce blood sugar levels, but that doesn't always work well enough—it's a very imprecise corrective. When diabetics die, it's usually because of the complications stemming from high blood sugar. The mystery with Baines was that he died with an incredibly low blood sugar level. Why was that, Mrs. Baines?" She was softly crying in a low moan.

"Did a nurse usually inject Mr. Baines with the insulin?" She let out a weak "yes."

"But isn't it true that you sometimes administered the insulin? And that maybe on that fateful day or night, you gave him too much—enough to kill him?" Now she broke into a loud, heaving cry.

"Ruth, you don't have to answer that question. The medical examiner ruled the cause of death as medical—diabetes."

"Yeah, Morgan, I wondered why the coroner was so quick to close the case," I interjected. "While Baines's low blood sugar level certainly wasn't conclusive evidence of a homicide, it was suspicious and deserved further investigation. But the police and the DA generally don't like to harass Hollywood and possibly kill the golden goose—and so they often look the other way when trouble occurs. And, of course, it's even easier for them to overlook bad behavior when money changes hands…."

"I never authorized any bribery—I wouldn't have had any reason to do it," Morgan insisted.

Mrs. Baines lit a cigarette and stood up. She looked like a demon: Her teary and angry bloodshot eyes were ringed with the blue-black of smudged and running eye makeup. She also exhibited a newfound demonic energy.

"Stop it. Stop it. Stop it," she said, punctuating her points with her cigarette. "Stop your lying, Spencer. You do it so often and so well that I think you actually believe all of it—every last lie. I know I did, a long time ago, while we were having our affair. You kept telling me you loved me, and I kept believing it."

"Ruth, I really thought I loved you…at the time."

"No, you loved the idea of sleeping with a rich, older man's young wife. But even that wasn't as important to you as the top job at a movie studio. You kept insisting that I persuade George to take Viogram public and arrange it so you—his dear friend—became the chief executive. Of course, George refused again and again to give up his baby to corporate control. And then he got diabetes and became very sick…." She lowered her head and started sobbing again, but her pent-up energy didn't allow her to stay in that state for long—she had too much more to say.

"With George now bedridden, your pitch to me changed. 'He's going to die soon anyway,' you said, and 'so why not hasten the process a little bit? Why not give him too much insulin, and just let him die away peacefully? Then,' you promised, 'we could finally be together and pursue our dreams.' Ah, yes, pursue our dreams. What you really meant was "pursue your dreams of power in a corporate Viogram. But I refused to see the truth; I preferred to believe your lies—they made me feel happy. I so wanted to feel happy…." She was no longer addressing Morgan or me. She was looking to some judge, who nobody, not even she, could see. "And then I did that awful thing: I gave George three times his usual insulin dose…and he just drifted off to sleep and died." With that, she broke down into bawling and now shaking. Words struggled to emerge, and I thought I heard them put together the phrase "I'm so sorry."

In looking at and listening to these two, I found it easy to be more sympathetic to the woman. But maybe that wasn't entirely right—almost, but not entirely. In the end, they were both incredibly selfish people who would do anything to get what they wanted. Morgan would betray and murder for power; Mrs. Baines would do the same for love. Morgan would lie to fool others, while Mrs. Baines would lie to fool herself. The significant difference between the two of them was that Mrs. Baines could recognize what she had done wrong and express sorrow about it. Morgan wouldn't regret any misdeed—he'd just cover it up with more lies.

"Ruth, you know I never told you to give George too much insulin. It never happened," he said. "But I'm shocked and disappointed to learn that you, in fact, killed him—my best friend in the whole world. How could you, Ruth? I know you didn't love George, but I thought you at least admired and respected this great man. Hearing your confession was like a shot to my heart."

I actually recoiled when I heard him say that. Not only was he angering Mrs. Baines with another lie, but he was also provoking Fate—and you never wanted to do such a thing. She reached for her purse, pulled out a .32 revolver, and pointed it at Morgan.

"Ruth, have you lost your mind?" he begged, leaning forward in his chair.

"Yes, I did—a long time ago. And that's why I still love you, Spencer." She then pulled the trigger twice, hitting him in the neck—and the heart. Baines collapsed, heading to the floor, face first.

Mrs. Baines now looked as if she had fallen into a stupor, and I wasn't sure if she could hear anything. But I stood up and told her to drop the gun on the floor. She tossed it to the side, and I kicked it under the sofa to keep it hidden from unfriendly hands. I sat her down. I checked Morgan's pulse, and there was nothing there. He was a big nobody now. The catatonic Chairman of the Board wasn't much better off: She would have to stand trial for three murders—if she ever completely woke up from her stupor.

But I didn't have time to worry about sad Hollywood love stories and unhappy endings. I had to call the police before Norton returned with Julie. Once he spotted his leader lying on the floor, he would surely sic his mad dogs on me. And I wasn't even sure if they had had their rabies shots yet.

I reached my antagonist-in-chief, head LA detective Pascal.

"Brad, this is Matt Moulton."

"Well, it's the big dick. What's wrong now, Matt?"

"Plenty. Remember that Viogram slavery plantation in Beverly Hills I told you about?"

"Yeah." He suddenly sounded bored.

"Well, I'm there right now with a dead body on my hands. A murder victim."

That got a rise out of him. "Oh! Who does the body belong to?"

"It's Spencer Morgan, the chief executive officer of Viogram."

There was silence on the other side. Then, he whistled and said, "holy Jesus! You didn't shoot him, did you?"

"No. He was shot twice by Ruth Gettling Baines, the Viogram Chairman of the Board."

"The big steel lady?"

"Yep. Now, if you can't handle this, I can always call the Beverly Hills Police." I already knew his answer. Looking the other way for Hollywood didn't mean that he would close his eyes to good publicity for himself. This murder would generate headline stories that would keep mentioning the supervising officer in the case, one Brad Pascal.

"No, I'll be right out there. We can coordinate with Beverly Hills Police later."

"Good." I gave him the mansion's address. "But I need you to hurry, Brad. And bring plenty of heat. They've got a lot of muscle and firepower here, and they won't be happy when they find out what's happened."

"Where are you in the mansion?"

"The library upstairs. While you're here, you can look at other parts of the operation. Like the rooms they confine the black slaves in. You can't ignore that crime now."

"I guess not." Pascal finally surrendered to the authorities of truth and reality. "See you soon."

A few minutes later, Norton returned with Julie. She looked very unhappy to see me. I represented a freedom she didn't want right now—Hollywood and heroin seemed like appealing, or at least tolerable, slave masters to her. Her emotional state was a tragedy, but it wasn't in my department—I could do nothing about it.

Norton immediately headed to the Morgan body. When he turned him over and spotted the bloody bullet holes, his face went pale. "What in the world happened?" he asked Mrs. Baines, who continued to stare at the empty space above him.

"He suffered an accident," I said. "I called the LA police, and they should be here any minute now." At least I hoped it would be any minute.

"Well, I better get some more help."

"That won't be necessary," I said as I pulled out the .38 under my jacket. "Let's just wait for the police." I frisked him and then invited him to take a seat on the sofa farther into the room. He glowered at me, probably in part because he thought I was the one who eliminated his bread and butter.

"Who do you think you are, Moulton?"

"A dick caught in a dirty, smelly job."

Suddenly, the door opened, and a thug holding Julie's suitcase entered the fray. He sized up the situation quickly and produced a gun, which he then put to Julie's head. "All right, fuck face, put the gun down," he said, in his high-pitched voice. Mrs. Baines projected a deeper voice in her big gun scene. "Once more, put the gun down," he said, even louder.

It was an impossible standoff, with seemingly no right move. If I kept my gun, he might panic and shoot Julie. If I gave it up, he or Norton might shoot me, and Julie would still be doomed. I couldn't be the hero here.

But the thug looked nervous, as if he had never been forced to put everything—including his own life—on the line before. Thus, not surprisingly, he flinched at the sudden crack of rushed voices in the hall outside the open door. But he didn't have time to do anything more. Within seconds, maybe two, they were at the doorway with a distinct message, "It's the police, drop your guns." The goon immediately obeyed. The cavalry had come, and I was never happier. They flooded the room, in uniforms and plain clothes, with the last guy to enter being Pascal. He looked taller than usual, and that was probably my grateful imagination at work.

"Brad, you came just in the nick of time—you're my hero."

"Maybe I should be in the movies."

"Well, Viogram won't hire you—not now."

Chapter Seventeen

On the Super Chief train back to Chicago, the country rushed past my private bedroom window. But the clock wasn't having it: Time continued moving at its deliberate, measured pace. Tick, tick, tick went the clock as Julie silently cried out for a heroin fix in her bedroom, a few doors down. Tick, tick, tick crawled the time, which was Julie's main enemy right now. The longer it took to get her professional help and medication, the closer she would come to suffering the terrible physical and mental effects of the "cold turkey." Given enough time, she could even die. Suddenly, I began to feel that everything in the world was taking too long. The train. This case. My separation from Gina. Even my cigarette. It seemed to burn forever, and I became so impatient that I mashed it out halfway through.

About an hour—or was it a week—later, I decided to check on Julie and see if she wanted to go to the fancy dining car for dinner and drinks. I knocked on her door, but she didn't answer. I knocked again, and she slurred something in response. Finally, a few seconds later, she opened the door and backed in. I followed her. The room was clean and uncluttered, and the bathroom door was closed.

"What's up, Matt?" she asked nervously. She had a cigarette

in her hand, and she was moving it around in a manic manner. Her eyes looked shrunken and jittery, and dark pouches were taking form underneath them. She was paying a high toll for this passage through dope withdrawal.

"Do you feel up to going to dinner, sweetheart?"

She turned her back on me, apparently tiring of the probe I was conducting of her face. "No, Matt, I'm not really hungry." She dragged on her cigarette.

"But don't you want to change the scenery? It would be healthy for you to leave this room for a while."

"No, I don't want to see the world right now. It hasn't been very good to me. It can go to Hell." The back of her head leaning to one side, she seemed to be trying to listen carefully, as if sound would tell her what I was doing or where I was looking.

"Okay." I turned to go, but something caught the corner of my eye. It was a spot of brown leather material hiding under and behind Julie's black purse on the sofa bed. I stepped over to reach for it, and she reached for me with flailing arms and desperate pleas. "No, no, Matt, please no."

The brown leather belonged to a small, anonymous-looking case, and I knew what was in it even before I opened it. It contained heroin powder, a syringe, a lighter, a spoon, and a shoelace. It was everything she'd need for a fix, for that hungered-after high that relieved the pain of withdrawal and— I guessed—numbed the agony of life.

"Where did this come from? I scoured through your purse and your suitcase twice. I even stripped you bare and searched you from hair to toe. Now, how did it get here? Who gave it to you?"

I heard the slightest click behind me, but it didn't register as important while I was grilling Julie, trying to get the dope on the dope that seemed to come out of nowhere. The next thing I knew, I was on the floor fighting to breathe and struggling to see—someone had hit me in a very vulnerable spot, on my upper back just below my neck. Whatever he or she used was heavy and hard. After a short, laborious while, I started breathing again, and first light and then full vision returned to my eyes. I sat up and immediately realized that standing up would be too ambitious a feat for me right then. Julie loomed over in front of me, but I turned away from her to face my attacker. It was Norton, and he was holding a gun.

"Well, well, you've returned to life, Mr. Moulton. That's good. I'm afraid it's only going to be temporary, however." He looked dressed for the outside, as if he had just boarded the train. That was impossible, and so he was apparently readying to unboard—get off at the coming stop.

"What are you doing here? Is the Super Chief recruiting slave-master pimps now?" I could hear Julie breathing hard behind me.

Norton lowered his head and frowned. "Moulton, you're such an arrogant bastard, even when you find yourself on the floor at the point of a gun. If I were you, I would be begging me to spare your life."

"Would you now? But again pimp man, what are you doing here? Are you intending to kill Julie with more dope?"

"No, you're wrong. I'm taking Julie off the train to save her from people like you and her mother. I love her, and I alone can help her realize her dreams." He looked like someone whose mind and heart were racing, someone who had taken on much more than he could handle.

"But it appears that you're about to feed her more heroin."

"Sure. It relaxes her, helps her better focus."

"Would you call that 'relaxed and focused?'" I said, pointing behind me.

"No, it's not. But she's like that now because of you. You've upset her by taking her away from me. Denied her what she needs."

"Yeah, she needs you—for dope. I assume it was you who first forced this crap on her."

"Forced?" He smiled. "Let's just say that I encouraged her to try something that would help."

I laughed. "That would help Viogram?"

He raised his voice. "No, help her."

"You mean like it helps you? I'll bet you don't even take it." I was still sitting on the floor, but leaning forward with both hands on my lower legs.

"No, I don't take it. I don't need it," he said, with pride.

"So you feed it to her instead. Why? Because she's black and you think you can more easily get away with it? Because you believe no one will care?" I shook my head. "You should know that her mother cares deeply about her. And as head of a big mob in Chicago, she'll come after you. She'll catch you. And she'll kill you, making sure it's done with a maximum of pain. I've heard the stories, and they're backed by good sources. The mob will slowly cut you up piece by piece while you're still alive and breathing. First, it will remove your manhood, then your ears, your nose, your hands, your feet, and well, I think you get the picture, pal. It's horribly disgusting what they do to their enemies. But they don't care what anyone thinks. And you know what? It could happen tomorrow, next month, or ten years from now—whenever they find you. The mob never forgets. It never gives up. And this mobster mother is ruthless:

She won't buy any phony stories about love—she'll just act. She wants her daughter back now."

Norton didn't move, and he didn't speak right away either. He suddenly had a lot more to think about. "I don't know that I believe your story."

"Are you willing to take the chance that I'm lying?"

"Whether it's truth or just a lie, I won't have to hear it anymore if I just kill you now." He waved the gun around, as if that would quiet me down and reduce the volume in his mind.

"You know, I've seen your kind of story before—the ugly guy who pines for the beautiful, younger woman. Oftentimes, the guy's got wealth, and so he tries to buy her. But you can't do that because you're apparently not rich. So you undertake a different approach: Enslaving Julie with dope to keep her by your side. It's love by force. Yes, you're a real romantic, Norton, a regular Romeo." I wanted a cigarette, but I needed to keep my hands where they were.

I raised my voice to address the desperate lady behind me. "What about that, Julie? Do you want to continue being Norton's slave?" She didn't answer, but he did—tightening his grip on the gun.

My threats and taunts were a big gamble. They angered him so much that he could pull the trigger at any second. But they distracted him as well—he seemed more lost in thought than ever. And when Julie suddenly stepped up to him, begging for her fix, it added one more slight distraction that gave me my opening. In the second or two, his agitated eyes tried to gesture away Julie, I reached with my right hand for the small holster under my left pant leg, pulled out my equalizer—a derringer gun—and fired. I've been a dead shot since I was a kid, but this shot was drop-dead accurate—it penetrated Norton's heart and ended his evening plans, for eternity.

Julie screamed. With her hands over her mouth, she then bent down and started crying over her dear dope supplier's body, the very top part of which was lying in the bathroom doorway. If investigating police took a picture from just the right angle, they could capture Norton's head with a toilet bowl at his side. He didn't die alone.

Now, where was his heroin bag? Julie didn't bring it with her when she approached him a minute ago. So I went to the other side of the room to search and spotted it lying on the floor in a corner. I picked it up and stuffed it into my pocket. I also dumped out and looked over the contents of her purse, for the third time. I had to ensure that Julie couldn't do a dope fix, at least on this trip, under my watch.

But then I turned around and faced a much more desperate problem. Julie was watching me with Norton's gun in her hand, and it wasn't pointing my way. It was pressed against her head, her finger was on the trigger, and she was quietly crying. I fell into a state of calm panic. I wanted to act, but couldn't— rushing forward might force her to pull the trigger, or it might set off the gun by mistake. So I tried to slow things down with urgently sympathetic talk. I never spent so much energy doing nothing as I did during that crucial moment.

"Sweetheart, please don't do anything rash. This crap is not for you—look at how it's left you feeling," I said, softly. Though feet away, my hands reached out to her, trying to say what mere words couldn't express as well. "You have a lot to live for—probably even a future in Hollywood. If that happens, we'll go to Ciro's together and laugh about all this. Wouldn't it be great to laugh? Please, please, Julie, just put the gun down.

Everything will look better tomorrow."

Her crying stopped, replaced by a look of despairing resignation. If that was a surrender to suicide, she proved unable to carry it out. Her finger squeezed the trigger as her gun hand began to collapse. The gun fired, and she fell to the floor.

I hurried over to her and found that she was still breathing and not bleeding anywhere—it appeared as if she had simply fainted. But while she didn't take a bullet, a bullet left its mark. The gunfire apparently passed so close to her face that it scorched the area around her eyes and nose, leaving a misshapen blotch—a kind of map of pain— that disfigured her beauty. Would she still be able to see now? I didn't know the answer yet. She'd almost certainly live. But I wondered, would she survive?

As I went off in search of a porter, I was blaming myself for this horror show. Dropped the ball? I felt as if I had just dropped someone's baby. I was a careless, fumbling bungler. Why didn't I take Julie back to Chicago on a plane? It would have been faster than the Super Chief, and it would have given someone like Norton less of an opportunity to violently interfere with us. Why did I leave her alone with his gun? I should have packed it away immediately after putting him away. I felt as if I had taken her extremely vulnerable state for granted.

I found a porter, and he said he'd send medical help right away. He also confirmed that we'd be making a scheduled stop in another half hour. Thus relieved, I tried to stop beating up on myself. As the train went dark, sweeping through a long tunnel, I attempted to find my own protective passage. It wasn't true that I didn't take Julie's plight seriously enough. Through my experience with my beloved Gina, I was especially conscious of the difficulties a black woman faces in America, and that knowledge probably motivated and shaped my pursuit of Julie. But did that mean I took the case too seriously, and turned the whole thing into a personal crusade, as Pascal suggested?

That wasn't true either. I was a problem solver, not a crusader. And how many problems could be more difficult than your client's black daughter being forced into slavery and dope addiction by a movie corporation gone rogue? In a country with a long history of racial bias and exploitation?

Despite the many challenges, including several attempts on my life, I solved the case—I was bringing Julie back home alive.

Yes, her wasted and wounded condition was going to devastate and even enrage Mother Rose. I didn't know how I was going to handle that situation.

And yes, I was going to suffer some rotten nights going over what I did wrong.

But really, what more could I have done? I couldn't solve the race problem. I couldn't cure America's obsession with Hollywood and celebrity-hood. I couldn't identify Julie's psychological problems, much less treat them.

In the end, it all came to nothing, nothing more than this: I was just a dick, someone whose business didn't often produce happy endings.

I always knew who I was. But why was it so hard to live with that now?

Chapter Eighteen

Finally arriving at my final stop, the Fischetti headquarters, I felt both safe and insecure. While Viogram couldn't reach me there, the lady of the house could smoke me without a trace. Would Rose punish me for the current condition of daughter Julie, who had badly deteriorated during her time away, particularly in the hours under my watch? She was ring-eyed, shaky, and drawn, as if I had been starving her not only of her dope, but also of food itself. On the train, she kept trying to wash away the huge burn mark on her face. When that, of course, didn't work, she refused to hide the mark with makeup—she defied everyone to witness what fate, helped by her own hand, had done to her. So she also said no to combing her hair and changing her wrinkled and soiled clothes. I was bringing my client, a daughter, who had gone from a confident cover girl to a mumbling rag bag woman. As the delivery boy, I would make the perfect immediate fall guy for Rose's rage.

Rose's full-bodied English butler let us in, but his manner this time was so funereal that I couldn't tell if he was greeting me or sending me away. He devoted most of his attention to Julie and—of course—my gun. I handed him my .38, but I kept my hat: If I had to die, I wanted to do it in my sporty black fedora with the light gray band.

He brought us upstairs to a larger, darker room than the office of my first meeting with Rose. Two people sat in the gloom, one behind the other, at the head of a large table. When Julie and I entered, the two stood up, a dim overhead light revealing that one was Rose and the other was Josh, my roughhouse friend, the Warehouse Man. Why was he in this meeting?

Clad in what appeared to be blood-red eveningwear, Rose quickly stepped forward and cried, "Julie! Julie?" A transparent wall then seemed to stop her cold. Despite my phone call warning her about Julie's condition, she looked totally shocked by her daughter's appearance. Julie's manner didn't help either: She acted like an immovable, sweating iceberg. Finally, after the long, uncomfortable pause, Rose rushed to her daughter and embraced her. Mother's warmth was enough to melt even Julie, who began to cry into Rose's chest.

"Oh, Julie, Julie, Julie, how could all of this have happened? It's unacceptable!" shouted Rose. She then looked at me with narrowed eyes and spat out that "this is an outrage!" She held Julie and stroked her now ratty-haired head for about a minute more before guiding her into a nearby chair. I felt as if I now had three judges facing me with a possible death sentence.

I sat down, lit a cigarette, and took a long, bracing drag. "Mrs. Fischetti, if you brought me my son or daughter in this condition, I would be as outraged as you are. But let's not forget that Julie must bear the immediate responsibility for at least that terrible burn mark on her face. As I told you on the phone, she tried to kill herself and narrowly missed, with the gunfire then singeing her. It's probably no solace to hear me say that the result could have been much worse, but it's undeniably true—you could have been measuring Julie for a diamond-studded coffin right now. If Julie ever stops feeling sorry for herself over her agonizing Hollywood experience, she'll realize how lucky she's been."

Looking at Julie, Rose sadly shook her head and reached over to grasp her daughter's hand. Julie quickly withdrew it. The mother-daughter reconciliation didn't look so promising after all.

"As to Julie's having been enslaved and drugged, a rough justice has prevailed over the people responsible. First of all, Stewart Morgan, the chief executive of Viogram and the guy who oversaw the black-sex slavery service, died of unnatural causes."

My revelation relieved some of the tension in the room. Rose brightened and almost smiled. "Did you kill him, Mr. Moulton?"

"No, I did not. His corporate boss, the chairwoman of the board, was the one who plugged the guy. She didn't appreciate his slavery business, among other things. Their relationship was a battle for domination—a love affair turned so ugly that it dragged innocent others into the fray, including Julie."

My attempt at an explanation seemed to find a receptive audience in Rose, who knew well about the mix of love and business and how especially volatile and explosive it can get when race—specifically racism—becomes an ingredient. Meanwhile, the lost Julie looked past me as if she were searching for something. Was it the heroin fix that wasn't there, or was it Michael, the innocent, who didn't make it? As for Josh, he just tightened his striped black tie and looked ominously impatient with me.

"Finally, Mrs. Fischetti, there was Ralph Norton, the

Viogram pimp who forced drugs on Julie and essentially put her in the state that you see her in now." I talked with the cigarette in my mouth because I didn't want to interrupt my verbal momentum with individual drags. The smoke swirled into my weary, watery eyes.

"You didn't really know him," murmured Julie. "I loved him... kind of."

"I didn't know him? Well, I knew he had a gun in his hand and planned to kill me. And I knew that he was going to return you to drug addiction and forced Hollywood prostitution soon afterwards. So I had no choice but to put a hole in him." I finally took my drag.

Julie banged on the table, which was more life than I'd seen from her since the train. Rose frowned at her and then smiled at me. "Bravo for your work, Mr. Moulton." Josh's eyes smiled, too, though I sensed that he was disappointed at how my story ended.

Though the room was hot, Julie started to shiver. She sat on the edge of her seat and looked around as if she was about to go do something significant—she just didn't seem to know what that should be.

Her confusion seemed infectious—her mother sat momentarily paralyzed before this new Julie, an unfamiliar state for the mob matron.

"Mrs. Fischetti, I don't want to detain you any longer. You need to find Julie some good medical care as soon as possible, a hospital that can gradually wean her off the smack. I'm no expert on dope withdrawal, but I think her life is in serious jeopardy right now."

Julie coughed and struggled to clear her throat. "Oh, okay, so they save my physical life. But then, what about my mental life?

What are they going to do about that?" She looked dreadfully out of sync: Her eyes were racing even as the words barely crawled out of her mouth.

"Don't worry, dear, I'll get you the best of everything. You'll stay right here and get well," said Rose, returning to her characteristic tone of hard, fast, and now.

"No, that's the problem, Mother. It's always everything under your control. I'm just one more thing you own." As I watched Julie violently shaking her head, I became even more sympathetic toward her. She wasn't really free here either. I took her from corporate slavery to mob-maternal incarceration. It was captivity with love. That was much better—wasn't it? I tried to tell myself it was.

"Now, we come to you, Mr. Moulton." Rose looked down at her folded hands. "We have to make sure you get what's coming to you—and then some.

"I owe you my gratitude...and a great deal of money," she said, her voice emphasizing the latter.

"Yes." I shook my head and gave her a toothy smile. She was going to let me live and even pay me to do it. I felt relieved and almost unworthy. Almost.

As Rose stood up and went to the wall safe behind her, Josh rolled his eyes, folded his hands, and exhaled. Unfortunately for him, she wouldn't need any of his action tonight.

She returned to the table with loads of cash. First she counted out on to the table ten one-hundred bills. "Now, what do I owe you for expenses, Mr. Moulton?"

"Oh, I don't know, say two hundred dollars?"

"Let's make it four." She added them to the pile.

"Now, I want to give you a bonus for eliminating that filthy slime-bag pimp. What was his name?"

"Ralph Norton."

"Yes, Norton, who's now pimping in Hell. For him, I've given you ten thousand dollars," she said, with satisfaction. She laid a band of C-notes next to the pile.

I stood up and reached for the pile—and left the band of ten thousand dollars sitting there. "I'm sorry, Mrs. Fischetti, I don't kill for cash. Uncle Sam paid me to be an assassin in France during World War II, and I despised the job, despite his appeal to patriotism. What's your pitch—just the money? I can't accept it. Even if I didn't have my moral qualms about that kind of killing, I'd be concerned about the law. I could be charged with murder for taking your money. So thanks but no thanks." I rubbed out what was left of my cigarette.

Rose looked confused and a little angry. What was wrong with her cash? Wasn't it as green as any other? How could a guy she so carefully hired act so ungratefully? Meanwhile, Josh just stared at me with his mouth wide open. However, he did have nice teeth.

I shook their hands and then walked over to Julie, whose head was lying on her arms across the table. I bent over and kissed her head and heard a choked wail. I guessed it was the sound of pain, confinement, injustice, hunger, boredom, and rage. It was existential and sadly familiar.

I couldn't take much more and so I disappeared from the room, vanished from the building, and faded away into the Chicago night.

About the Author

After dropping out of high school and later having nothing to his name but a GED, Michael Amedeo began writing. The active voice helped him earn a BA in Political Science from the University of Illinois at Chicago and an MA from the intellectually demanding University of Chicago. He became an award-winning creative copywriter for corporations and agencies, a freelance film critic and journalist for several newspapers and magazines, and a PR and media relations writer for still more organizations. Looking for a new writer's edge, Amedeo turned to fiction and used his hardboiled *film noir* background to create the stylishly embittered private dick, Matt Moulton.

AUTHOR WEBSITE:
  michaelamedeo.com

Also by Michael Amedeo

Past Tense: A Matt Moulton Mystery

www.ingramcontent.com/pod-product-compliance
Lightning Source LLC
Chambersburg PA
CBHW050447110726
47899CB00003B/840